MIRR

GEMINI

(May 22 to June 21)

Sensitive and highly strung one minute, flirty and funloving the next, Gemini is the most versatile sign of the Zodiac. Totally unpredictable, Geminis are quite capable of leading a double life, putting on whichever mask they choose. They can always see two sides to everything but this can make them doubly cautious in everything they do.

Gabrielle is a popular pupil at White Springs Academy, a school she thinks of as her home. But when she has to return to her childhood home for the funeral of her parents, a very different Gabbie emerges. She becomes out of control, malicious and trusts no one. Is Gabbie a schizophrenic or has her body been taken over by an evil spirit?

Whatever your sun sign, you'll want to read Zodiac, the series written in the stars.

ARIES (Mar 21 to Apr 19)	SECRET IDENTITY
TAURUS (Apr 20 to May 21)	BLACK OUT
GEMINI (May 22 to June 21)	MIRROR IMAGE
CANCER (Jun 22 to Jul 22)	DARK SHADOWS
LEO (Jul 23 to Aug 23)	STAGE FRIGHT
VIRGO (Aug 24 to Sep 23)	DESPERATELY YOURS
LIBRA (Sep 24 to Oct 22)	FROZEN IN TIME
SCORPIO (Oct 23 to Nov 21)	DEATH GRIP
SAGITTARIUS (Nov 22 to Dec 21)	STRANGE DESTINY
CAPRICORN (Dec 22 to Jan 19)	DON'T LOOK BACK
AQUARIUS (Jan 20 to Feb 19)	SECOND SIGHT
PISCES (Feb 20 to Mar 20)	SIXTH SENSE

SERIES CREATED BY JAHNNA N. MALCOLM

GEMINI

MIRROR IMAGE

JAHNNA N. MALCOLM

Lions
An Imprint of HarperCollins*Publishers*

First published in Lions in 1995

Lions is an imprint of CollinsChildren'sBooks,
a Division of HarperCollins*Publishers* Ltd,
77-85 Fulham Palace Road, Hammersmith, London W6 8JB

1 3 5 7 9 8 6 4 2

ISBN: 0 00 675050 8

Printed and bound in Great Britain by
HarperCollins Manufacturing Ltd, Glasgow.

Special Thanks to
Coleen Hubbard

CHAPTER ONE

GEMINI (May 22-June 21)

Moon in Cancer indicates an emotional roller-coaster at home. But remember, Gemini and Janus have two faces, so you can put on whichever mask you choose. You'll be wringing your hands over something in your life that will prove a turning point. This is an enigmatic transit, signifying double-dealing, double-edged sword, double trouble or double blessings.

"There's been a terrible accident. Both of your parents are dead. I'm so very sorry."

Gabrielle Bradford heard Mrs Albion's words but couldn't understand how they could possibly relate to her. She blinked her wide brown eyes at the headmistress of White Springs Academy. "Excuse me?"

Mrs Albion rose from behind her big walnut

desk and poured a glass of water at the antique side table. "Drink a glass of water, Gabrielle. It will make you feel better."

Gabbie sat stiffly in the tapestry chair in front of Mrs Albion's desk. Her hands were clasped tightly in her lap. So tightly that her knuckles had gone white. "I feel fine." Gabbie's lips moved and words came out of her mouth, but they had nothing to do with the cold hand of fear that had suddenly gripped her insides.

Mrs Albion looked the very picture of a prim white-haired headmistress in her navy-blue suit with a cream-coloured blouse and ruby-encrusted pin at her throat. She set the crystal water glass on her desk and patted Gabbie on the shoulder, trying to offer her some comfort. But comfort had never been Mrs Albion's strong suit. Politeness and manners were what she could offer her girls. And discipline. Never any real warmth.

"There, there," Mrs Albion murmured, as if Gabbie were crying.

But no tear stained Gabbie's cheek. She stared intently at a heavy cut-glass paperweight, the only ornament decorating the severe wooden desk, and wondered what emotion it was filling her insides and causing her heart to beat faster.

"Fear," she murmured to her reflection. "I'm scared."

"Well, of course," Mrs Albion said, satisfied that she had somehow been able to get Gabrielle to respond to the terrible announcement. "That is a perfectly natural reaction. Don't try to bottle up your emotions. Just let them out. You'll feel better."

Gabbie, who had been mesmerized by the myriad images of her own frightened reflection in the paperweight, looked up at Mrs Albion. "Better?"

"Of course." Mrs Albion pushed back her chair behind her desk. "If you let yourself have a good cry, it will help you deal with this terrible news."

Deal with the death of both parents? Gabbie wanted to laugh out loud. How could anyone deal with that? To be part of a family one moment, and the next be told you're an orphan? Impossible. "Your aunt is sending a car for you," Mrs Albion continued. "It should arrive within the hour. Would you like me to go back to your room with you and help you pack?

"No, thank you." Gabbie stood up. *Where's the door?* Nearly twelve years at the White Springs Academy and she couldn't remember where the door to the headmistress's office was. She turned in a circle on the oriental carpet. Rows of books filling the floor-to-ceiling walnut shelves whizzed by. The heavy tapestry drapes shrouding the windows looked dark and foreboding. Maybe there wasn't a door. Maybe she was trapped.

Gabrielle continued to spin. *Maybe this is a dream. My parents aren't really dead. This isn't really Mrs Albion's office. I'll wake up soon.*

Mrs Albion got up from her desk and touched Gabbie's arm, stopping her spinning. "Gabrielle, you're in shock, no doubt. As well you should be. But please remember we have a counsellor on our staff. Dr Brehoney has worked with a number of the girls at White Springs Academy who have experienced a loss of some kind."

Gabbie looked Mrs Albion square in the face, wanting to laugh out loud. This wasn't a loss "of some kind". This was gargantuan. Overwhelming. Devastating. But Gabbie didn't laugh. Twelve years at the academy had hammered the proper veneer of politeness into her head.

"May I be excused?" was all she managed to say.

"Of course, my dear." Mrs Albion placed one hand on Gabbie's back and guided her towards the door, which was carved of thick oak, standing prominently between two bookcases. Gabbie wondered how she could have missed it.

"Please let me know if there's anything I or the staff can do for you," Mrs Albion said, ushering Gabbie into the reception area and giving her a brief hug.

Gabbie submitted to the hug, then turned and marched across the thick grey carpet past Mrs Kirk, the secretary, who was busy typing at her desk. Mrs Kirk paused long enough to give Gabbie a sympathetic smile, which Gabbie acknowledged with a nod of her head.

Gabbie walked stiffly towards the door leading out of the administration building, her school uniform of blue and green plaid wool skirt, white blouse and blue blazer rustling crisply with each step. She wanted to run, but so many years at White Springs told her she needed to maintain her poise, at least until she was outside.

Once at the doors, Gabbie flung them open and ran. She'd always preferred running to walking and today her feet pounded as fast as her heart. She fled from the stuffy, rose-scented office, with its porcelain teacups and framed awards. The cold marble foyer with its long parade of faded black-and-white photos of past graduates, whom she'd never met and never would meet because they were probably long dead. Gabbie leapt off the white pillared porch and darted past a group of sophomores from Mr Potter's Biology class, who were gathered on the front lawn studying leaves.

The other one hundred and twenty students at White Springs were either still in classes in Carpenter or Livingston Hall, or at the field house for the afternoon athletics programme. Gabbie was mercifully alone, running across the lush green commons of the academy.

The dogwood and cherry trees lining the grass were in full spring bloom. Everything was pink and white, bursting with vitality. Alive. Gabbie breathed in the heady floral scent and tried to fill her insides with colour. But something dark and very cold would not let it in.

"Gabbie! Wait!" a voice squeaked from across the commons. Gabbie slowed to a stop and turned. Her best friend Liz Sutton was jogging towards her. Instead of the school uniform, Liz was dressed in riding clothes. The chin strap of her riding hat flapped against her neck as she ran and her red hair stuck out in all directions from beneath it, like a bright frizzy fringe.

"Oh, Gabbie, I just found out." Liz flung her arms round Gabbie and cried, "God, this is terrible! I'm so sorry!"

Now I should cry, Gabbie thought, as her friend held on to her, weeping. But still the tears wouldn't come.

"How did it happen?" Liz asked, wiping at her eyes with the back of her sleeve. "When did it happen?"

Gabbie ran both hands through her short, spiky dark hair. "I don't know, Liz. Mrs Albion just said there'd been an accident."

"A car accident?" Liz took Gabbie's arm and walked her through the slender dogwoods towards Smith Hall, which was their dorm.

"I didn't ask," Gabbie said, her eyes widening in surprise. "Can you believe that? I didn't even think to ask."

Liz squeezed her arm. "It's OK that you didn't ask. Don't worry about it."

But Gabbie was worried. First she couldn't cry, and now it seemed she didn't even care enough to ask how her mother and father had died. "What's the matter with me? Why didn't I ask?"

Liz hopped in front of Gabbie, her short, slightly pudgy figure blocking her way. "You've had a major shock. An overwhelming shock. You're probably too upset to think clearly about anything."

Gabbie listened to her best friend's words and shivered. She was upset – but not sad, like everyone expected. Something cold and dark had crept into her thoughts and was frightening her.

Gabbie bent her head and whispered, "Liz, I know this may sound weird, but I'm scared."

Liz hugged her. "Of course you are."

"No." Gabbie shrugged off her friend's embrace. "I mean, *really* scared."

Liz cocked her head. "Of the future?"

"Yes," Gabbie replied. "And no." She tugged at the ends of her hair just over her left ear, which was a habit she had when she was deep in thought. "I'm not afraid of what will become of me, though I guess I probably should be, since I'm really alone now. But I'm scared of. . . something."

"You're not alone," Liz said, earnestly. "I'm always here for you. Always."

Liz stuck out her little finger and Gabbie linked fingers with her. The two chanted the vow they'd made in eighth grade, when the two of them became best friends. "Through thick and thin, through dark and light, no one can break our bond so tight."

This time Gabbie's eyes did fill with tears. Not because of her parents. But because of Liz, and how much she meant to her.

"Come on." Gabbie gestured towards Smith Hall. The squat brick building with its dark green shutters (nicknamed Toad Hall by the girls) housed fourteen of them, plus one house mother. It had been Gabbie's home since she moved from the younger girls' dorm in junior high. "Help me pack. Mrs Albion said my aunt is sending a car for me in less than an hour."

"Where will you be going?" Liz asked as they hurried up the steps.

Once again Gabbie stopped and frowned. "I didn't ask. Isn't that weird? I assume I'm going to my parents' home. Aunt Louise must be there."

"Aunt Louise?" Liz glanced at Gabbie one eye shut. "I think I've heard you mention her before. But how long has it been since you've seen her?"

Gabbie pursed her lips. "Twelve years."

At Liz's look of surprise, Gabbie reminded her, "We were never a very close-knit family."

The two girls stepped into the main hallway of the house and practically ran into Mrs Carruthers, their house mother.

"Oh, my poor, poor Gabbie," the very round woman exhaled as she wrapped her big, comforting arms round Gabbie. Everything about Mrs Carruthers was soft – her voice, her fluffy brown hair, her heavy body. Even her meals were soft – great heaped plates of formless Southern food like hominy grits, mashed potatoes, sweet potato pie, bread pudding and fresh peach cobbler. "My heart just aches for you."

Gabbie patted Mrs Carruthers on the back gently and murmured, "It's OK." It was strange. She was supposed to be the grieving orphan but so far Gabbie was having to comfort everyone else.

Mrs Carruthers dabbed a tear from her eye and smoothed Gabbie's short, spiky hair away from her face, flattening it down. Usually that was irritating to Gabbie, but today she didn't care.

"I'm sure Liz can help you pack," Mrs Carruthers murmured. "And I'll put together a snack for you to eat in the car. You need to eat, Gabbie, and keep up your strength. I know how you forget to eat when you're under stress, you poor thing."

Gabbie cringed. The staff at White Springs was always calling her "poor dear" or "poor child" or "you poor little thing". They meant it with affection. But it only reminded Gabbie that she had been in residence at the academy longer than any other girl, and that her parents rarely visited.

Gabbie and Liz climbed the narrow stairs to the first floor. Their room was just off the landing. Suddenly Gabbie got that cold, jittery feeling again. She stopped on the landing to take a deep breath.

"Hey – are you OK, Gab?" Liz asked.

"Just a little shaky inside," Gabbie confessed. "I have this weird feeling about the future." She added with a chuckle, "Maybe I should check my horoscope."

Liz cocked her head. "You did. You read it this morning. Remember?"

"Of course." Gabbie leaned her head against the wallpapered stairway. "I totally spaced it. It said today would be a turning point for Geminis."

Liz whistled low. "Boy, were they right about that."

"But it also said I would have something lost and something gained." Gabbie shook her head. "I've lost my parents, but what have I gained?"

"I don't know," Liz pushed her frizzy red hair out of her face. She loved to read about astrological signs, and was considered the resident horoscope expert by the girls in Smith Hall. "But you're a Gemini. The twins. There has to be a flip side to this tragedy."

"I wish I could believe that." Gabbie took a

key out of her pocket and moved to the top of the stairs. Their room was the first one on the right. She unlocked the door. "But I have this terrible premonition that things are going to get worse before they ever get better.

CHAPTER TWO

Word of the disaster spread fast. Within the hour, nearly twenty girls had stopped by Gabbie's room to offer sympathy and hugs.

When her room finally emptied, Gabbie returned to watching Liz pack. For some reason, Gabbie couldn't bring herself to open one drawer or remove a single item from her wardrobe. She let Liz do everything.

"Gabrielle! *Ma pauvre* Gabbie!" a voice shouted from the entryway downstairs.

Liz and Gabbie looked at each other. "Darby."

Darby Kent was their roommate and one of the most outlandish students at White Springs. She had been off campus for the afternoon and was among the last to hear the tragic news.

She hurried into the room carrying a Styrofoam cup of steaming hot coffee. "Here, I brought you some coffee," she said, presenting

Gabbie with the cup. "I always want coffee when I'm sad."

Gabbie stared at the coffee, certain she'd throw up if she drank it. "Thanks, Darby. I really appreciate it."

Darby, who had dyed her hair a violent shade of maroon the week before, perched on the windowsill and lit a cigarette, making sure to blow the smoke out the window. "This is all *si triste.*"

"You're telling me," Liz muttered as she tucked several of Gabbie's T-shirts and slacks into the suitcase.

Darby waved her cigarette in the air. "*Mon Dieu*, I just feel so helpless. I mean, is there anything I can do?"

Gabbie stared at the cup of coffee, mesmerized by the rising steam swirling into the air. "There's nothing anyone can do. They're dead."

Darby took a drag of her cigarette, and exhaled loudly. "I meant for you, *ma cherie*."

Liz had her back to Darby and rolled her eyes in Gabbie's direction. Ever since Darby's trip to Paris the previous summer she had sprinkled her sentences with snippets of broken French.

Today she was on overload.

"Look, Darby, why don't you watch for the limo?" Liz suggested, moving to the chest of drawers. "Gabbie said it's supposed to be coming for her soon."

"They're sending a limo?" Darby waved her cigarette dramatically. *"C'est magnifique.* I'll stand guard and sound the alarm when I see them." She took a final drag from her cigarette and then stubbed it out in an old tin can she kept hidden under her bed. Darby blew the remaining smoke out the window, and then dropped her flamboyant façade. "Gabbie, you shout if you need me for anything," she said simply. "I mean anything – I can carry a suitcase, or just stand here and be a strong shoulder to cry on."

Gabbie smiled at her outlandish friend. Beneath all the silly posturing beat a good heart. "Thanks, Darby. That means a lot to me."

In true Darby fashion she kissed Gabbie on both cheeks, then hurried downstairs to take her post at the driveway.

After she left, Gabbie set the untouched coffee on her bedside table and wandered round their room, touching things. She quickly found her favourite stuffed animal, a bear named Edward, and set him gently on top of the folded clothes in her suitcase. Though he was missing an arm and an ear and was bald in patches, Gabbie had loved him since she was a baby.

She picked up framed pictures from desks and stuffed animals from each girl's bed. It amazed her that within one room there could be three such distinct decorating styles.

Her own bed was covered in a quilt that Liz's mother had given her. On top of it lay several needlepoint cushions she had made during the long vacations when she had stayed at the school while the other girls had gone home to visit their families. Scattered on the low table beside the bed were several novels Gabbie had started but never finished.

She really was a true Gemini – or at least that's what Liz was always saying. Never able to concentrate on one project. Her bookshelf held the watercolour paintbox from the time when she had decided to become an artist. Next to the paints was her knitting bag, containing a half-finished sweater. And on the lower shelf sat a black leather case holding a shiny new flute.

Liz's bed and desk showed her to be a true Sagittarius. Despite her round figure, she was a real athlete. Her book shelf was crammed with sports biographies and riding trophies. The wall above her desk was lined with red, white and blue ribbons from riding competitions, as well as posters of soccer and baseball stars.

"I love this room," Gabbie murmured, picking up one of Liz's horse trophies. "I love your awards, and the copy of *Misty of Chincoteague* that is always under your pillow, and your desk with the secret compartment for m&m's and midnight snacks."

"That compartment was your idea," Liz reminded her as she folded a long-sleeved floral print nightgown and tucked it into Gabbie's suitcase. "As were those hollowed-out books where we could leave each other top secret notes."

"I love my beaded friendship bracelet that you made for me the first week we met," Gabbie said, taking the plaited circlet off her bulletin board and slipping it on to her wrist. "I used to pretend it would bring me good luck."

"It will," Liz said mysteriously. "I had a special charm put on it."

Gabbie sunk on to her bed with shoulders slumped, surveying their room. Her eyes misted over and there was a catch in her voice as she said, "I love my lamp with the burnt shade, and your lamp that your brother made you out of recycled bottles. I even love Darby's posters of Paris – though sometimes I feel like I'll scream if I hear her mutter one more *mon Dieu*!"

"Ditto!" Liz said, moving to Gabbie's wardrobe and taking out two dresses on hangers. She held them side by side in front of her, debating whether to pack the purple silk or the deep red knit. "But what about Darby's obnoxious cigarettes?"

Gabbie shrugged. "They're such a part of her that I even love them."

"You talk as if you're leaving Smith Hall for ever."

"I feel that way," Gabbie murmured as she crossed to the window. Dark clouds were gathering in the east and the air had the sudden smell of rain. The hair on Gabbie's arms stood up for no reason at all. "And it terrifies me."

Liz marched over and, putting her hands firmly on Gabbie's shoulders, spun her round. "Now listen here, Gabrielle Bradford. A very terrible tragedy has happened in your life. But it's over. Nothing more is going to happen to you."

"I wish I could believe you," Gabbie whispered.

Before Liz could say another word, Tiffany Randell stuck her head in their room. "Gabbie, I heard."

Liz groaned under her breath, "Oh, great. It's Miss Insincere."

Tall and athletic, Tiffany Randell was known for her competitive edge and biting sarcasm. She ranked as one of Gabbie and Liz's least favourite people.

Tiffany stepped into the room. "Was it political?"

"Was what political?" asked Gabbie, confused.

"Your parents' death. I mean, they were in Central Africa, in a war zone. It had to have been political."

Gabbie wanted to explain that her parents had been back in the States for several months, but then Tiffany, not to mention everyone else, would wonder why they hadn't been to visit her. It was always easier to be evasive.

"I'm not really sure. I think it was a car accident," Gabbie replied.

"In Washington?" Tiffany continued to probe.

Liz, who had returned to her packing, slammed Gabbie's drawer shut. "What does it matter, Tiffany?"

Tiffany recoiled. "I was just curious, Liz. You don't have to snap my head off."

Liz knew she'd gone over the top. "I'm sorry," she muttered hastily. "We're just having to hurry here. The limo should be arriving any minute.

"A limo?" Tiffany raised one eyebrow. "Well, at least you get to take one last ride at the taxpayer's expense."

This time Liz really let loose. "What a jerky thing to say!"

"It was a joke."

"Well, no one in this room is laughing. And for your information, practically every girl at White Springs is here on federal money. You included."

It was true. The posh White Springs Academy catered to the daughters of US ambassadors and other foreign service officers stationed in remote or dangerous parts of the world where good schools were not available. The US government not only paid for them to go to school but also to fly off regularly to visit their parents. Tiffany's father wasn't in the state department but a senator from Texas, which only added to her heightened opinion of herself.

"Well, excuse me," Tiffany huffed. She shook her blonde ponytail. "I was just trying to be nice to Gabbie, but apparently I'm not wanted here." She spun on the heel of her tennis shoe and marched out of the room.

"Good riddance," Liz muttered. She put her hands on her hips and smiled at Gabbie. "I've put two days worth of clothing – two dresses, jeans, T-shirts, a nightgown, underwear and make-up – in this suitcase. Anything you want to add?"

Gabbie picked up a recent photo of her parents. It showed her mother and father posed in front of an official US government Jeep, somewhere in central Africa.

"This was Dad's last assignment," she told Liz. "Ambassador to some banana republic with bad water and an awful civil war, just like Tiffany said."

"Don't pay any attention to Tiffany," Liz said, with a wave of her hand. "She flunked social skills in a major way."

Gabbie stared at the photo. "My parents are practically strangers to me."

"Your parents are – were a little weird," Liz murmured.

"That's the understatement of the year," Gabbie said with a humourless laugh. "I've spent more time with your mom and dad than I ever spent with mine."

"You're part of my family, Gabbie," Liz said, handing her a framed picture from her desk. It showed the two girls with Liz's parents and two brothers in front of the Sutton home in Philadelphia. "We all love you."

Gabbie hugged the photo to her chest and then gently placed it in her suitcase. "What would I have done without your family all these years? Think of all the weekends and holidays I've spent with them."

Hot tears rose in her eyes as she thought back on her lonely years at White Springs, before she met Liz. How many times had she seen her parents? She could practically count the visits. Occasionally, a birthday. One graduation, several school programmes. They never had her to visit them in Africa, even when it was scheduled by the school. They had rarely answered the weekly letter she was required to write while living at White Springs. Even when they had been reassigned to the States, they hadn't arranged for Gabbie to visit them.

Gabbie shut the suitcase hard and spun to face Liz. "Why do you think my parents hated me so much?"

Her question took Liz by such surprise that she could only stammer, "They – they didn't hate you. I mean, how could they? You're beautiful, and smart, and funny—"

"Obviously they didn't think so," Gabbie interrupted.

Liz shrugged. "Think how much they travelled. Think of all those awful places they were assigned to. Maybe they thought you'd be better off here. Safer."

Gabbie was unconvinced. She blew her nose into a clump of tissues and moved back to look out the window. A stab of lightning zigzagged in the distance. *I guess I'll never know.*

Liz finished tidying up Gabbie's side of the room. As she stacked Gabbie's school books on to her bookshelf a photo slipped out of one of the books. "I've never seen this," she said, handing it to Gabbie.

The picture had been torn in half. The remnant showed a dark-haired little girl walking between a handsome young man and his pretty wife. Gabbie studied the picture carefully. "This is the only photo I have of me with my parents. Can you believe it? I think I must have been about two or three years old. See? I'm holding my mother's hand, which was a rarity."

"What's this?" Liz pointed to the edge of the photo. "It looks like someone else is walking beside your father."

Gabbie examined the picture. "It does."

The ragged edge of the tear angled down her father's left side, cutting off his hand. But it was clear from the angle of his arm that he was holding another, much shorter person's hand.

"But who's little hand could it be?" Liz asked.

Since the picture was torn, there was no way of knowing. All Gabbie knew was that the picture made her shiver, not just from cold but from a nameless, paralyzing fear. She quickly slammed the photo face down on her desk.

Beep-beep!

"Gabrielle!" a voice called from outside on the lawn. "*Votre voiture, c'est arrivé.* Your car is here."

Gabbie looked out the window and saw that a sleek black car had pulled up to the kerb. A crowd of girls lined the driveway. It wasn't an unusual sight to see a limousine at White Springs – students were often chauffeured. The girls were merely waiting to say goodbye to Gabbie, to act as formal "ambassadors" of the school, paying their respects.

Gabbie made a small, strange cry like a wounded animal. "I don't want to go, Liz! Please help me. I want to stay here!"

"You have to go," Liz said as she lifted the suitcase off the bed. "You can't skip your parents' funeral – no matter how you feel about them right now. Now take a deep breath. Geminis store all of their pain in their lungs. Breathe!"

Gabbie did as she was told. She closed her eyes and tried to breathe in enough air to quell the panic starting to churn inside her.

"Remember, Gabbie," Liz whispered, "you are a Gemini. Your ruling planet is Mercury –

the messenger to all the other gods. Just listen for messages and you'll be OK."

Gabbie took several more deep breaths, and then followed Liz out of the room.

"Call me tonight," Liz instructed Gabbie as they moved down the stairs. "Let me know what the funeral arrangements are so I can tell my parents. They'll want to go, I know it. Don't worry, Gabbie, you won't be alone."

The two girls walked out the door of Smith Hall and on to the stone pathway. The air was growing thick from the coming storm and Gabbie struggled to catch her breath. The girls grouped by the limousine parted to let them through.

As the limousine driver stepped forwards to take Gabbie's suitcase, thunder boomed over their heads and rain began to fall. Mrs Carruthers hurried over to Gabbie with the promised snack in a white box tied with a pink ribbon. She hugged Gabbie and said, "We're here, honey, if you need anything."

Her father's assistant stepped out of the car. Gabbie wasn't very surprised to see him. Over the years, Terry Leaming had often handled personal business for her father – including issues regarding his only daughter.

"Hello, Gabrielle," Terry said. He was dressed in a sombre black suit, and his long face looked sad.

"Hi, Terry."

"Are you ready?" he asked, looking at her with affection.

"I guess I am," Gabbie answered.

Gabbie stepped into the back seat of the limousine. But as soon as she was seated she cried out of the open window. "Liz?"

"What?" Liz leant down to peer in at her.

"Colin. I was supposed to go to a movie with him on Friday."

"Don't worry, I'll call him. Do you want him to come to the funeral?"

"No. Absolutely not." Gabbie was adamant. She and Colin had only been dating for about a month. Their relationship was nice and casual. Gabbie wasn't ready to share her twisted relationship with her parents and their sudden death with him. It would be too hard.

"I love you, Gab." Liz bent and kissed Gabbie on the cheek. "Remember that."

Liz started to stand up, but Gabbie clutched her arm, whispering so no one could hear. "Oh,

Liz, I have this horrible feeling. . .that if I go there – to that house – nothing will ever be the same again."

Liz's reply was lost in the sound of crunching gravel as the limousine pulled away from White Springs Academy.

CHAPTER THREE

Gabbie waved out of the tinted glass window until her friends were just dots on the landscape. When she could no longer distinguish them or the faded brick buildings of White Springs Academy, Gabbie turned towards Terry Leaming. She was hoping to ask him specific questions about her parents. But before she could open her mouth the car phone rang. Soon Terry was deep in conversation with someone about diplomatic business.

Gabbie leaned back against her seat and watched the countryside roll by as they headed for Maryland.

Thirty minutes later, Terry hung up. Gabbie started once again to ask the questions that were burning in her mind. *What happened to my parents? When did it happen? What will happen to me?* But the phone in the car continued to ring. With every call Terry talked repeatedly about “releasing pertinent information to the international press” and “timing the announcement of a diplomatic replacement”.

Finally, after nearly an hour had passed, there was a quiet moment. Terry smiled at Gabbie apologetically. “I’m sorry, Gabrielle. This is all so—”

“It’s OK,” she told him. “And call me Gabbie. That’s what everyone at the academy calls me. Except for Mrs Albion, of course.”

“Your father always referred to you as Gabrielle,” Terry explained. “But then, he was a rather formal man, wasn’t he?”

“I guess,” Gabbie said. *As if I knew. You knew him lots better than I did, believe me.*

“I talked to your parents only a few days ago,” Terry said, shaking his head. “They were so excited about moving back to the old house. Your mother said she only wished they’d done it sooner.”

“It’s been boarded up for ever,” Gabbie told him.

“I know. Had you been back since they began the renovations?”

“Renovations?” Gabbie was surprised. No one had mentioned anything about redoing the house. Her mother had written her a brief note, saying, "We're returning to our home." Their home. Not hers. "I haven't seen that house since I was five," she confessed. "I always saw my parents at their town house in Georgetown."

"Well, let me tell you, it's a gorgeous estate."

"You've been there?" Gabbie asked, trying hard not to look as if her jaw was completely dropping.

"Several times," he replied. "Your parents invited me up for a house-warming barbecue the day they moved in, and then your father and I had a few business meetings this past week. He—" Terry's voice caught in his throat.

Even her father's assistant was more upset about her parents' death than she was. Why did she feel nothing? Gabbie laid her head back on the seat, wishing Liz were there. At least Gabbie would be able to say, "See? I told you they didn't love me. They had a house-warming and didn't invite me. Only an hour and a half away and they didn't want to see me."

"Gabbie, there's something I think I should tell you." Terry paused, struggling for the right words.

"What is it?" Gabbie raised her head.

Something about the look on Terry's face made the fear start churning inside her again.

Terry held his black leather appointment book in his lap. He nervously flipped the corner of the cover as he spoke. "I know you're used to being in the public eye, after all these years of being an ambassador's daughter."

"Actually," Gabbie interrupted, "my parents kept me very sheltered from all that. I was almost always at school."

"Then you were lucky," Terry said, knowingly.

"Lucky." Gabbie frowned. She had never thought of herself as lucky. In fact she considered herself pretty unlucky where life was concerned. And this recent turn of events proved it.

"Anyway," Terry continued, "when we arrive, you should be prepared to encounter a few reporters, and probably even a detective or two."

"Detectives?" Gabbie asked. "Why?"

Just then the car turned up the long driveway leading up to Bradford house. It was bordered by massive poplar trees, and the fine white gravel crunched underneath the tyres. A police car came out of the driveway, just as they turned in. It drove slowly past.

Gabbie felt clammy and her heart was beating fast. She stared up at the magnificent house as the limousine came to a stop. Set high on a ridge overlooking the Potomac River, the house had a commanding, almost looming appearance. Four white wooden pillars held up the massive overhanging porch, which bordered the entire front of the house. The angle of the sloping roof was broken only by two dormers on the first floor, opening on to two delicate-looking, white wooden balconies connected by a widow's walk.

"Does it look the way you remembered it?" Terry asked.

Gabbie turned to Terry and shrugged. "I don't remember it at all."

Sure enough, as Gabbie got out of the car, a reporter with a huge camera practically jumped on her. He seemed to come out of nowhere. "Hey!" she yelled, temporarily blinded by the flashbulb in her face.

"Leave the child alone," Terry roared. He came round and stood protectively by Gabbie.

"How do you feel about your parents'

death?" the reporter asked, not backing off.

"How do you think she feels?" Terry snapped. His voice had a stony edge that made Gabbie flinch. Still the reporter didn't budge.

"Have you talked to the FBI?" the reporter continued. He snapped a picture of the house. "Has the girl given a statement?"

Gabbie looked at Terry for an answer. "FBI? Statement? What's going on?"

"I'll have to ask you to leave now," Terry told the man firmly. The photographer snapped several more shots, then finally left on foot.

"I'm sorry, Gabbie," Terry apologized. "The press can be extremely obnoxious."

Gabbie didn't really hear him. She was staring up at the wooden balcony. She could tell that a portion of it had broken away, or was in the midst of repairs. It was obvious that her parents had been restoring the place, for ladders and paint supplies were stacked on the porch. And it looked as if the roof was new. Someone had even begun to dig a garden plot on the north side of the house.

"Did Mother garden?" Gabbie couldn't ever remember discussing the subject. Of course, that wasn't unusual. Her mother had always managed to say as few words as possible to her.

"Yes, I believe she did," Terry said. "I know she liked flowers and made herself responsible for the arrangements that decorated our offices."

It was hard to picture her mother in gardening gloves, cheerfully arranging vases of flowers. That would be too pleasant.

"Let's get you inside, Gabbie." Terry took her elbow and guided her towards the porch. "Before any more reporters find this place."

"They've really made a mess of the lawn," Gabbie remarked, picking up an empty film canister and a piece of orange plastic that looked like police tape. The grass was badly trampled in a broad patch directly below the first floor balcony.

"That's part of their MO. Destroy everything in sight." Terry said wearily. He'd obviously dealt with one too many pushy reporters during his tenure with the foreign service.

Gabbie put one foot on the porch and froze. Although the nearest neighbour was half a mile away, she heard a dog howling quite close by. It was an eerie sound. Even Terry stopped in his tracks and listened.

"Probably a warning," she murmured. "Don't go in there."

Before Terry could reply, the front door swung open, and a tall woman dressed in a long black skirt and sweater stepped outside. She looked vaguely familiar.

"Hello, Gabrielle," the woman said, keeping her hands clasped firmly in front of her. "Do you remember me?"

"Aunt Louise," Gabbie replied. It had to be her. She looked like a clone of Gabbie's mother, except a little thinner and much older. Louise's dark hair was peppered with grey and drawn into a bun at her neck. Everything about her seemed cold and stern.

"It's very nice to see you," Gabbie lied. She actually felt just the opposite. She didn't remember much about Aunt Louise except the feelings her aunt stirred inside of her. Loneliness. Despair. At some point in her life she had spent time with this aunt and had been utterly miserable.

"I see you've grown into a real beauty," Aunt Louise said, studying her carefully. "You're still a careless dresser." She directed her stare at Gabbie's shirt-tail that had come untucked at her waist. "But then as a child you were always sloppy."

Gabbie felt like she'd been slapped in the face. She didn't really expect anything from her aunt except a little kindness, and that was the one thing she wasn't getting. *But why? What did I do?*

Terry Leaming came to her defence. "Mrs Palmer, Gabbie is tired and has suffered a tremendous shock."

"As have we all," Aunt Louise replied. Although her voice was even with self-control, her chin quivered as she spoke. It was clear that her sister's death had been hard for her to accept. Gabbie's aunt stared at her hands for a moment. "But you are right, Mr Leaming," she said finally. "I'm not being very hospitable. Please come inside, Gabrielle. I'll make you a cup of tea. You must be exhausted."

"Thank you, Aunt Louise," Gabbie said, stepping across the door sill. "I do feel very—"

Her words died in her throat as she was struck by an overwhelming sense of familiarity. Everything smelled of fresh paint and newly sanded wood floors, but she knew this place.

"Terry," she gasped, as her aunt hurried off to

get the tea. "I remember this house." She pointed to her left. "The dining room is over there. The kitchen is at the back. There's a bathroom on the main floor, and a tiny cloakroom off the kitchen."

Testing her new found memory, Gabbie tiptoed round the first floor. Even though most of the rooms were bare of furniture and still stacked with brown packing boxes, Gabbie had flashes of old paintings, upholstered sofas, and antique furnishings.

"This is so bizarre," she murmured to Terry, who had perched on the edge of a couch and was watching her. "Ten minutes ago I couldn't have told anyone a thing about this house. Now I remember practically everything. Even the furniture that used to be here."

Aunt Louise returned, carrying a silver tray that held the tea service. She set the tray on the table and said, "Gabrielle. Why don't you take your things up to your room, and wash for tea."

"My room?" Gabbie repeated. Was it possible her parents had actually made a room for her? "Which one is that?"

Aunt Louise stared at Gabbie for a long moment. "The pink room, upstairs, to the left.

Don't you remember?"

"I'm not sure," Gabbie answered, truthfully.

"Would you like me to carry your bag up for you?" Terry offered.

Gabbie chuckled. "No. I'm fine. There are only a few things in it. As you can tell, it doesn't weigh a thing." She picked up the suitcase and moved to the stairs. Behind her she could hear her aunt speaking to Terry as she poured tea. "Normally, the household staff would be here to help, but since the accident they've refused to return to their jobs."

Gabbie began to ascend the stairs to the upper floor. But with each step, she was filled with a growing sense of dread. As she got closer to the top, her heart raced faster and faster. At the landing Gabbie had to stop. She closed her eyes and took a deep, calming breath.

When she opened her eyes again – suddenly, she remembered. Her bedroom, the pink one, was in the right front dormer of the house. Gabbie knew the wallpaper would have tiny pink roses on it, her bed would have a pink canopy, and her dresser would be white with a pink rose painted on each drawer.

But there was another room. Identical to hers

but with a different colour to the rose decor. "The yellow room," Gabbie murmured.

Gabbie turned to move towards it but was suddenly frozen in the corridor, caught between the two rooms.

"Pink. I want pink."

"No, yellow."

"Pink is best. Pink is my favourite colour. I'm taking the pink room."

The tiny voices engaged in the argument seemed to be coming from inside her own head. Gabbie dropped her suitcase and clutched at her temples, trying to make the voices go away.

"Stop it!" she shouted. "Just stop it!"

Her scream seemed to break the force and she was able to run for the safety of her bedroom.

But once inside, Gabbie was hit with a blast of frigid air, as strong and bone-numbing as frost from a deep freeze. She hugged her arms tightly round herself and shivered uncontrollably. Then a sickly, sweet stench filled her nostrils. *I think I'm going to be sick.*

Gabbie bolted from the room, one hand covering her mouth and the other clutching her stomach. She took the stairs two at a time and raced down into the living room, where her aunt and Terry were having tea.

"What's the matter?" Terry asked, setting his cup back in his saucer with a clatter. "You look like you've seen a ghost."

Gabbie trembled and clutched Terry's arm. "I didn't see a ghost, but I sure felt one."

Terry put one hand over hers to comfort her and his eyes widened. "Gabbie, your hands are as cold as ice."

Gabbie nodded. "It's freezing up there."

"I'm sorry about the heat," Aunt Louise said, getting to her feet. "I should have turned the furnace on earlier. Who would have thought it'd be so chilly at this time of year?"

Gabbie looked at her aunt, and at Terry. "The kind of cold I felt can't be fixed with a heater."

"What do you mean, Gabbie?" Terry asked.

She struggled to put her horrifying new knowledge into words. "It felt like death itself."

CHAPTER FOUR

When Gabbie woke up on Friday morning, she didn't know where she was. As she gradually surfaced from a troubled sleep she began to remember. She was lying on the couch in the living room of her parents' home in Maryland.

"My parents," Gabbie murmured, untangling herself from the knitted orange-and-yellow afghan she'd draped over herself. "The funeral. It's tomorrow." Gabbie got off the couch, still holding Edward the stuffed bear, and shuffled towards the east windows. The sun streamed brightly through the glass, stinging her eyes that burned from lack of sleep.

After her experience in the pink room, Gabbie had decided there was no way she would sleep upstairs. No matter how she tried, she couldn't shake the feeling that someone – or something – evil was lurking there. The house had been full of people all evening, coming and going, tying up her father's affairs, finalizing the preparations for the funeral. So it was quite late when Gabbie crept downstairs and slipped into the living room. She'd found some photo albums and stayed up leafing through them. It had been fascinating, yet saddening to see the rich, full life her parents had led, and to realize how little she had been a part of it. The sky had already begun to lighten in the east when she finally dropped off to sleep on the couch.

Gabbie glanced up at the grandfather clock against the wall. It was quite late, almost eleven o'clock in the morning. She tiptoed into the kitchen, wondering where her aunt and Terry were. Aunt Louise had graciously accepted Terry's offer to stay with them until her husband Lawrence arrived. Aunt Louise had made up the guest bedroom for Terry, and put herself in the master bedroom.

A half-empty pitcher of orange juice sat on the kitchen counter, along with a plate of muffins and the morning paper. Gabbie poured herself a glass of juice and reached for the paper. *I'll read my horoscope – that would make Liz happy.* She flipped through the paper, bypassing the real news, until she reached the entertainment section.

"Aries, Taurus, Gemini," Gabbie muttered, running her finger down the side of the astrology column.

Stay focused today, Gemini. You'll need all your powers to cope with things brewing behind the scenes. Don't let your energy be drained by your tendency towards distraction. Strong friends will help you cope.

Strong friends. *Liz!*

She hadn't had a chance to call Liz the night before. Now would be the perfect time. Gabbie shut herself into her father's study on the ground floor, where she'd noticed a phone the night before. She didn't want to be overheard by Aunt Louise or Terry. They'd been sticking too close to her. Ever since her scare in the pink bedroom.

Gabbie looked round the small, stuffy office. Mostly, it was filled with unpacked boxes, like the rest of the house. But someone had taken the time to put framed pictures on the walls and to set up several bookshelves. The desk was a mess. The drawers were pulled open and their contents in a jumble. It almost looked like someone had been rummaging for something.

Gabbie dropped into her father's heavy walnut office chair with its rich leather upholstery, and picked up the receiver of the old-fashioned black rotary phone. She dialled her dorm room and Liz answered after one ring. She sounded relieved to hear from Gabbie.

"I've been going crazy trying to reach you," Liz told her. "My parents need to know the time of the funeral. I said I'd find out but I didn't have your phone number. And it's unlisted."

"My phone number is—" Gabbie held up the phone, looking for the number which should have been printed on the dial. She shuffled through a few of the papers on the top of her father's desk and then blew her fringe off her forehead in frustration. "I can't believe I don't know my parents' phone number."

"Didn't they just move back there?" Liz asked.

Gabbie swivelled her father's chair to face the panelled wall. "Well, yes, but you'd think I'd be one of the first people to be given the number. Not the last."

Liz, who had spent many years listening to Gabbie complain about her parents, murmured a sound of sympathy, then changed the subject. "So when is the funeral?"

"Three o'clock tomorrow, at St Martin's in Prescott. Do you think you can make it?"

"My parents are driving down in the morning. They said to tell you we'll be there."

Gabbie smiled. "They are so great."

"They also told me to tell you that they'll take us to dinner afterwards and, if you're up to it, give you a ride back to White Springs."

"Damn." Gabbie spun the chair back round and rested her elbows on the desk. "I can't leave here until Sunday. I'm supposed to meet with my aunt and uncle and a bunch of lawyers after the funeral." Even though she was alone, Gabbie lowered her voice and whispered, "I really don't want to stay here. This house gives me the creeps."

"I'd feel the same way," Liz agreed.

"I mean, there were people crawling round here until almost midnight. Terry – my father's aide – and my aunt. Making arrangements. And for some reason, the police have been here. And photographers."

Liz's voice suddenly sounded worried. "You must be really freaked out because of how your parents died. I wouldn't have even been able to sleep there! You're so brave, Gabbie!"

"What do you mean, freaked out by how my parents died?" Gabbie repeated. "What are you talking about?"

"Oh, my god!" Liz gasped. "You mean you don't know? It's been all over the papers and on television. I thought you knew!"

"I haven't read the paper or seen any TV. What is it, Liz? Tell me."

There was a long pause. Finally Liz said, "Maybe I shouldn't tell you."

Gabbie sprang to her feet, angry. "If you know and the whole world knows, then don't you think *I* deserve to know, Liz? You're supposed to be my best friend – now tell me!"

Liz's voice was small and quiet. "They were found dead on the path in front of the house. They. . .they were in their nightclothes."

The trampled grass. The broken balcony upstairs.

"I-I don't understand," Gabbie stammered. "Did someone break in?"

"I heard on the news last night that the police

found no sign of a forced entry."

"But if they were shot—?"

"I didn't say that," Liz interrupted.

"Then – how did they die, Liz?"

Gabbie braced herself for the answer, but suddenly the line went dead.

She rattled the phone and shouted into the receiver. "Liz? Liz? Answer me!" She slammed the phone back on the hook and that cold, eerie feeling filled her once more. Slowly Gabbie looked up from her father's desk and saw her Aunt Louise standing in the doorway, watching her. Her aunt's face looked like she'd just caught Gabbie smoking – or worse.

"I didn't hear you come in," Gabbie said, standing up. She began to tidy the scattered papers on the desk.

"Who were you calling?" her aunt asked. Her voice was heavy with suspicion.

"My friend," Gabbie said evenly, forcing herself to smile.

"I see." Aunt Louise continued to stare at Gabbie. She reached a hand up to fix a few loose strands that had fallen from the tight knot of hair gathered at her neck. She was wearing black, just like yesterday. "Please let me know if you need to make any more calls," she said stiffly.

"If you're worried about the phone bill, I have my own charge card," Gabbie said, starting to feel pretty indignant. "But it really shouldn't matter. I mean, this is my house. Isn't it?"

Her aunt ignored Gabbie's question. "There's a man here to see you. He's from the FBI."

"FBI?" Gabbie repeated, confused. "Why?"

"He would like to talk to you about your parents," her aunt replied. "It's too bad you're dressed like that. Your mother would have been appalled."

Gabbie looked down at her jeans and wrinkled T-shirt. She'd slept in her clothes on the couch. Gabbie touched her hair, which she hadn't had a chance to comb. "I just woke up."

Her aunt checked her watch. "It's after eleven. The rest of us have been up for hours. There's still so much to do before tomorrow's funeral."

"And Terry?" Gabbie interrupted.

"At the office in Washington. He was amazed, as were we all, that you could sleep so soundly. Under the circumstances."

So that's it. Her aunt was upset that Gabbie could appear to be so casual about her parents' death. How could she know that Gabbie had spent the night fighting demons from her past in the dark? But she wasn't about to share that information with her aunt. Instead she said, "We all have different ways of dealing with grief."

"Of course." With that, her aunt left the study. Her heels clacked rhythmically as she walked away down the parquet floor of the hall.

"Excuse me," said a male voice. In the door stood a man in a dark blue business suit. He extended a hand. "I'm Ron Scharfe, Special Agent, FBI."

The man looked familiar, and Gabby realized he had been at the house briefly the night before. In all the confusion, they hadn't been introduced. "Hi. I'm Gabbie Bradford."

"My condolences, ma'am. I just have a few questions I'd like to ask. Do you mind if we take a walk outside?"

Gabbie followed him, noting his dark suit and short, conservative haircut. Just like in the movies. Why did government agents always wear dark suits?

They walked out of the front door on to the

broad expanse of lawn stretching towards the road and the curving Potomac beyond. A gigantic oak tree shaded the right side of the lawn and garden furniture had been set beneath it, making a pleasant place to view the river. The chairs were still covered in protective canvas cloths. Agent Scharfe sat down in one and motioned for her to join him.

"Nice place your family had," he said, gesturing to the view. "Did you grow up here?"

Gabbie remained standing by the tall oak. "I guess I lived here till I was about five. But I don't really remember those years." She absent-mindedly gave a push to an old tyre swing hanging from the lowest bough. The morning air was still cool, and fragrant. She took a deep breath, listening to the thud of the rubber tyre bouncing against the trunk of the massive tree.

"This would be a great place for a kid to grow up," Agent Scharfe continued, but Gabbie didn't hear him. Her head was too full of a new set of voices.

"I want to go first!"

"You always get to swing first. It's my turn!"

"No, it's mine!"

"Miss Bradford!" An impatient voice broke through Gabbie's thoughts. She blinked her eyes, realizing she hadn't heard a word he'd been saying.

"Yes?" Gabbie rubbed her temples. Where were those voices coming from? They blasted through her brain as if broadcast from a loudspeaker.

"I was asking when was the last time you visited this house?"

"I'm sorry." Gabbie shook her head. "I haven't been here for twelve years."

"Twelve years!" The agent seemed surprised. "But it's my understanding that your parents moved back her nearly a month ago."

"That's what Terry Leaming told me," Gabbie replied, still rubbing her temples.

The agent made a few notes on a pad, then looked up at her. "How would you describe your relationship with your parents?"

As a non-relationship, Gabbie wanted to reply. Instead she thought for a moment and said, "Formal."

"Formal." Agent Scharfe knitted his eyebrows together. "Kind of an odd word to choose."

Gabbie sighed. "Yes, but I think it's the correct one. 'Warm' certainly wouldn't fit. 'Cold' would be more accurate. But that would imply that we'd had some sort of disagreement, which we never had. We weren't close enough to fight. That's why I think formal is the right word. Or polite."

He scribbled furiously for a few moments, and finally said, "How do you feel about your parent's death?"

Gabbie threw her arms in the air impatiently. "Why is everyone asking me how I feel about their death? How do you expect me to feel? Great?"

"I'm sorry," Agent Scharfe replied. "But I have to ask."

Too little sleep and too much stress over the past twenty-four hours finally caught up with Gabbie. "Ever since I arrived at this house, I've been under a magnifying glass. My aunt criticizes the way I sleep and dress, you ask me ridiculous questions about whether or not I'm upset that both my parents have died. What's going on?"

The muscle in Agent Scharfe's jaw clenched several times before he responded.

"We're simply trying to conduct an investigation. Your parents died under very...peculiar circumstances."

"That's another thing." Gabbie gave the tyre one more tremendous shove. "No one bothered to tell me anything about their deaths. I only found out this morning that they died here at the house."

"That's correct." His eyes narrowed slightly as he watched her. "Their bodies were discovered on the front path."

"But I don't even know how they died." Gabbie could feel her face heating up with anger. "Why won't anyone tell me what happened?"

"I can tell you what I know," Agent Scharfe replied quietly. He flipped to the front of his spiral notebook and read out loud. "The coroner reports that they died on impact. The position of their bodies indicates that they fell from the balcony outside their bedroom."

"The balcony?" Gabbie snapped her head up to look at the first floor. Part of the white railing was broken. *That's where they must have broken through.* Beyond the railing, she could just make out the tops of three wicker chairs grouped round a wicker table. Something was propped up in the middle chair, peering over the table like a small child.

"What is that?" she said, pointing.

The agent followed her gesture. "It's a porcelain doll."

"Doll?" Gabbie's insides did a flip-flop. The cold, dark chill that had gripped her before came rushing back like a tidal wave. Gabbie shivered so hard that her teeth chattered.

"Do you know anything about it?" the agent asked.

Something clicked in her mind for a second – something about the porcelain doll. Then it was gone. "No. I don't know anything." Gabbie rubbed her temples again. "I just can't believe they could accidentally fall off that balcony."

"Your parents didn't fall," Agent Scharfe said quietly. "They were pushed."

CHAPTER FIVE

Transiting Moon in melancholy Capricorn dampens your spirit. But you, Gemini, can always see both sides of the coin, so keep your head and wits about you. The next few days may be rough but sunshine always follows the rain. And remember – one door closes, another opens.

"We are gathered together today to say farewell to Ambassador Nicholas Bradford and his wife Susan Fitzgerald Bradford. A doubly sad day for all who knew and loved them. . ."

Gabbie sat in the front pew of the country church, trying to focus on the minister's words, but her mind kept drifting. The church was stuffy and packed with strangers. Mostly government dignitaries.

She scanned the crowd, looking for familiar faces. Terry Leaming was there. So was the

Vice-President's wife, whom Gabbie had met once. There were a few other faces she recognized from pictures in the paper but that was about it. The President of the United States had sent a huge arrangement of flowers and a card with a wax seal. That held the place of honour between the two caskets.

"We are met in this hallowed place," the minister continued, "to say goodbye. . ."

They're saying goodbye, but I never said hello, Gabbie thought. This whole funeral only served to make Gabbie realize once again how little she knew about her parents, and how few friends she had.

Where is Liz? Gabbie peered behind her. The stiff waist of her dress was scraping her skin and she squirmed uncomfortably. Liz and her family were wonderful people but they did have one flaw – they were always late. Today was no exception.

Gabbie's aunt saw her squirming in her seat and shot her a "Sit still!" glare, as if she were a small child. It had been like that from the moment she'd arrived at her parents house in Maryland. On Friday afternoon her aunt had sent her to the nearest town to buy a suitable black dress for the funeral. The small village of Prescott had exactly two dress shops, one of which, the Villager, happened to have a black knit shirtwaister in Gabbie's size. She bought it despite the fact that it itched, even in the dressing room.

Friday night had been a replay of the night before. She'd made excuses that she wanted to sit up and read, and eventually fell asleep on the couch. At some point during the night someone had awakened her. She was certain it was her aunt shaking her shoulder but, when she flicked on the light, no one was there. Then towards morning those voices, the ones she had heard arguing in her head, came back.

"I'm hiding, I'm hiding, and you can't find me."

"I don't want to find you," she'd murmured, nearly delirious from lack of sleep. When her aunt roused her in the morning, it felt as if she'd only been asleep for ten minutes.

"Get up and get dressed." Aunt Louise was her usual warm self. "Your Uncle Lawrence is here. You should say hello before we leave for the church."

She didn't remember her uncle at all. But

now they framed her in the pew like two severe bookends – the thin balding man with glasses on her left, and the stern, humourless woman on her right. Aunt Louise, Gabbie's only living relative. *My family. All that's left of it.*

One by one, a dozen people got up to deliver personal tributes to her parents. They spoke of "courage" and "commitment"; "integrity" and "patriotism". They told stories of her father's work round the world and of her mother's social graces and selfless work for charities. Gabbie was fascinated by what was said, which filled in some of the many gaps in her knowledge of her parents.

Gabbie was relieved that no one had asked her to speak. What could she have said, except that her parents had been great travellers? She had collected quite an exotic postcard collection as a result of their globetrotting. The postcards seldom served as more than travel itinerary updates: We're in Paris now. We will return in a month. Mother.

Liz. Wonderful, supportive Liz had decided that Gemini, the explorer, would keep the cards as a guide for future travels. Together they assembled a "wish" book with additional cards of their own. Gabbie's side was filled with postcards from the most exotic locales like Bali and Machu Picchu. Liz, the Sagittarian, had chosen photos of the English countryside, and anything that was good horse country.

"Let us bow our heads."

As the minister led the mourners in a prayer, Gabbie felt a sharp rap on her shoulder. It was more like a punch – the way kids at school get one another's attention during class.

Liz! Gabbie turned round quickly. But no one was there. The pew behind her was empty. Everyone else in the church had their heads bowed in prayer.

Who did that?

Gabbie spotted the FBI detective, Ron Scharfe, standing near the back of the church by the wall. He, too, was carefully watching all the people in the room and jotting notes in his notebook.

Gabbie wondered if he was looking for suspects. *Maybe murderers go to the funerals of their victims the same way pyromaniacs stay to watch the fire they've started.* Could the person who murdered her parents be sitting innocently here among the mourners?

Gabbie turned round and tried to concentrate on the prayer but the room was getting stuffier, and the scratchy dress was making her skin crawl. Her mind kept wandering back to her conversation with Agent Scharfe that morning.

He had told her there hadn't really been any sign of a struggle. "The only thing at all out of the ordinary was the three glasses of milk, half-consumed, on the table on your parents' balcony. And a plate of cookies – lemon cookies."

"My favourite," Gabbie had replied. "We used to drink milk and cookies as a late night snack before bed."

"When?" he'd asked.

Gabbie couldn't remember. "When I was younger. But they rarely ate lemon. Their favourite was chocolate chip."

The agent seemed to take special note of that. When Gabbie asked who was drinking the third glass of milk, Agent Scharfe didn't know. "Your parents were found in their nightclothes," he said. "So it had to be someone they knew well enough to be pretty relaxed with them. But so far we're clueless."

"Could they have been having a snack with

the maid or butler?" Gabbie had suggested.

"Obvious first choice," he'd agreed. "But they were both off that night, with airtight alibis."

Gabbie loved to read mysteries, which, as Liz put it, was "a true Gemini trait". Her bedside table was usually piled high with the latest P.D. James or Martha Grimes. Her mind started clicking like the detectives in her novels.

"I would start with their close friends," Gabbie told the agent. "Have Terry Leaming put together a list."

"I've already asked him to do that," the agent had said. "But I'd like you to make one, too."

"Me?" Gabbie had chuckled. "You probably know more about my parents than I do." She told him briefly the story she most hated to tell. That she rarely saw her parents. That she spent most holidays and summers either at the academy or with Liz's family.

"That would explain why I had no idea your father even had a daughter," the agent said.

"Hardly anyone knows about me," Gabbie said ruefully. "I was their little secret."

Their secret. Their invisible daughter.

"One last question," the agent had said.

"Where were you the night your parents were murdered?"

"At school, of course."

"I'll be talking to your headmistress," Agent Scharfe had said, almost apologetically. "Just routine, you understand."

Gabbie had read enough detective stories to know that he would. When the FBI man had finally driven off in his unmarked government car that morning, Gabbie breathed a sigh of relief.

Now here he was again, back in her world.

"Nearer my God to thee. . ."

The first notes of the closing hymn jolted Gabbie back to the present. People all round were blowing their noses and wiping their eyes. The minister invited the people to pay their final respects.

He means view the bodies! Gabbie was suddenly filled with panic. She didn't want to do it. At Liz's uncle's funeral, she'd almost fainted walking past the open casket. From where she was sitting, she could see her parents just fine. They looked like wax mannequins, asleep. Her father's thick black and silver hair showed above the creme coloured satin of the casket. Her mother's fine dark hair was beautifully coiffed. Her make-up, perfect. Gabbie didn't recognize the dress but her mother's ever-present gold necklace with its double-heart locket glinted in the candlelight.

The locket! Gabbie straightened up in her seat. Throughout her entire life she had never been permitted to look inside that locket. Now it would be buried with her mother. She'd never find out what secret it held.

Aunt Louise was the first to approach the caskets. She sobbed loudly, clutching at her husband Lawrence. To Gabbie's horror, Louise leaned down and kissed her mother's face. Then she turned and gestured for Gabbie to join her.

Oh, no! Now I have to go! I have no choice!

But as Gabbie got to her feet, she felt the dizziness begin and the voices return.

"Me first."

"No, me."

"You always go first."

"That's because I'm better than you."

Then Gabbie felt her arm being gripped tightly. Nails dug into her flesh. She yanked her arm away, yelling, "Stop it!"

People in the church stared. Her aunt, still

standing at the casket, looked shocked.

Terry Leaming was instantly at Gabbie's side. He put an arm round her shoulders and whispered, "Are you all right?"

"I – I think so. What happened?"

"You shouted 'stop it'," Terry told her gently.

Gabbie tried to mumble an excuse. But she couldn't shake the sensation of her arm being gripped hard, and of someone punching her on the shoulder. And what about those voices in her head?

"It's OK," Terry whispered. "Sometimes funerals make people do odd things. Don't worry about it."

Gabbie's cheeks burned with embarrassment. Her temples throbbed. But she was determined to endure the viewing. Head down, she approached the caskets. Gabbie felt a slight pressure on her elbow and silently thanked Terry for his support. She felt herself being guided towards the caskets. They were ringed by wreaths of flowers, many of them pink.

Once by the caskets, Gabbie wanted to stop and look. Say goodbye. She tried. But in the confusion, people pushing and jostling in front and behind her, Terry's hand guiding her firmly, she found she couldn't stop. Her feet moved past the caskets, through the crowd, and out of the church.

A misty spring rain was falling. Gabbie took a deep breath and turned to Terry. He wasn't there!

"Terry?" she murmured. "Where are you?"

Her aunt and uncle were the next to leave the church, followed by the minister. Gabbie heard her aunt say loudly, "This proves it. Did you see her sail past her parents without a second glance? That girl has ice-water in her veins. Always has. Wouldn't even pay her respects to her own parents!"

A fierce anger boiled inside Gabbie. How dare her aunt talk about her like that!

The cold darkness filled her body. Colours from the church's stained-glass windows swirled in front of her eyes. She yanked at the collar of her dress, trying to pull it away from her skin. Gabbie opened her mouth to speak, but she had no control of what came out. Then there was nothing – except for the feeling of falling. Falling down a long, dark tunnel.

When Gabbie came to, a crowd of strangers surrounded her. Someone helped her to her feet.

Someone else pressed a wet handkerchief to her forehead. She saw her aunt being led towards a limousine by her uncle. Louise was sobbing uncontrollably.

Gabbie tried to follow, calling out for them. "Wait!"

But her uncle turned and the furious look in his eyes stopped her. "You ride with someone else," he hissed. "You've upset your aunt enough. We don't want you near us."

Something terrible had just happened. But what? Gabbie spun in a circle looking for a familiar face. No one, not even Terry Leaming, was in sight. The faces in the surrounding crowd reflected their disdain for what had happened, and they dispersed quickly, leaving Gabbie alone on the church lawn. She watched helplessly as her aunt's limousine pulled away from the kerb.

All round, the other mourners got in their cars to follow the hearse to the cemetery. Gabbie stood staring into the distance, feeling completely abandoned. She was on the verge of collapsing in total despair when she spied a familiar blue dot coming down the road.

"Liz!" Gabbie screamed as the Suttons' big

blue Lincoln turned into the church driveway. "Liz! Help me!"

Gabbie couldn't wait for the car to reach her. She stumbled down the centre of the gravel drive, waving her arms for Mr Sutton to stop. The moment he did, Gabbie flung open the back door and jumped inside.

"Please get me out of here," she cried, throwing herself in Liz's arms.

Liz hugged her. "We got lost, Gabbie. I'm so sorry."

"Is it over, honey?" Mrs Sutton asked, turning to stroke Gabbie's hair.

"Should we go on to the cemetery?" asked Mr Sutton. His voice was filled with fatherly concern.

"No. Anywhere but there." Then Gabbie, who'd been unable to cry throughout the long funeral, began to weep uncontrollably.

Mrs Sutton handed her a box of tissues from the front seat. "It's OK, Gabbie," she murmured. "Funerals are hard. You've had such a hard time, honey."

Gabbie was able to stop sobbing long enough to squeeze out a few words. "Please," she begged. "Take me home. Back to White

Springs. Please!"

Mr and Mrs Sutton looked at each other and nodded.

The rain fell in sheets now. Mr Sutton turned the Lincoln round and joined the long line of cars leaving the church. As they passed the hearse, Gabbie looked back for one last farewell and gasped.

A very familiar little dark-haired girl was standing by the hearse. She looked Gabbie straight in the eye and laughed. A wide-mouthed, terrible laugh.

"Who is that?" Gabbie rubbed at the fogged-up window with her hand to get a better look at the girl.

But she was gone. Vanished into thin air.

CHAPTER SIX

"I can't believe I'm home," Gabbie told Liz that evening. She pulled her blue terry-cloth robe tighter round her and cupped her hands round a steaming mug of hot chocolate. "Today was the worst day of my entire life."

"I don't think I've ever seen you so upset," Liz replied sympathetically.

The two girls were sitting at the kitchen table in Smith Hall. It was almost nine o'clock at night, and for the first time all day, there were no adults round. They were finally free to talk.

"I couldn't say anything earlier," Liz added, "but for a minute there, I really thought you were losing it."

Gabbie stared through the glass of the French windows at the back of the kitchen. "So did I. I'd reached the point where I was hearing voices."

"Voices?" Liz took slow sip of her chocolate,

then licked the moustache off her lip. "You mean, scary voices?"

Gabbie tugged nervously at one ear. "What they were saying wasn't scary. In fact it was more like little kids fighting. But it terrified me."

Liz set her mug down on the old wooden table. "Sometimes people hear voices when they're tired. How much sleep have you had?"

"An hour or two," Gabbie confessed, staring out the window at the rain. "Of course, my aunt thinks I spent my entire time at the house asleep."

"That witch." Liz got up to pour herself some more chocolate. "I can't believe she just left you standing on the kerb with all of those strangers. She should be arrested!"

Gabbie dropped her head back and looked at the kitchen ceiling. "If I never see her again it will be too soon."

"Unfortunately, you probably will have to see her again," Liz warned. "I mean, she is your only living relative. Although my father is going to talk to the authorities about her behaviour."

"I feel really embarrassed about how I acted

in front of your mom and dad this afternoon," Gabbie groaned. The thought of it still made her face burn.

"A murder is no easy thing to deal with," Liz said, slipping back into her chair. "Actually, my parents are amazed that you're doing as well as you are, considering what you've been through. By the way, did you see the pile of sympathy cards on your desk? Our mailbox was stuffed."

Gabbie nodded. "I don't think I can handle opening them tonight. And if I never see another flower arrangement, it'll be too soon."

Clunk.

The noise came from just outside the French windows. "What's that?" Gabbie cried, leaping to her feet.

"What?" Liz frowned at Gabbie.

"That noise." Gabbie stared at the darkness outside the windows. "Out there."

Liz got up from her chair and walked to the French windows. She opened one and peered outside. "It's just the rain hitting the garbage cans."

"Are you sure?" Gabbie asked, putting one hand to her face. She realized she was quivering.

Liz took Gabbie's hand and led her through the doors on to the tiny patio. Their bare feet slipped over the wet bricks. "See? It's nothing. Just the rain."

"You must think I'm an idiot," Gabbie whispered. "But I'm certain I heard something – and it wasn't the rain."

"That's because you are a Gemini," Liz replied, draping her arm over Gabbie's shoulder. "Geminis are highly strung. And jumpy. That, plus major lack of sleep, and you're going to hear and see things. You should probably go straight to bed."

"I'd love to," Gabbie sighed. "I've hardly slept at all."

The girls turned to go back in to the warmth of the kitchen. But as Gabbie stepped through the door, she saw a figure seated at the table, pale and ghostly. The head slowly turned to look at her.

"Oh, my god!" Gabbie covered her mouth to stifle her scream.

"What's wrong?" Liz cried, coming from behind Gabbie. The figure instantly dissolved.

"Someone. I – I thought I saw a girl at the table." Gabbie clutched her middle, afraid she was going to be sick. The face, pale and ghostly, was somehow familiar. But whose was it?

"Let's splash some water on your face," Liz said, guiding her to the sink. "Boy, you're starting to make me jumpy."

"Liz," Gabbie murmured after running cold water on her cheeks and forehead. "Something very strange is happening to me. Ever since I walked in to that house in Maryland, I've had the feeling that I'm not alone."

"You mean, like you're being followed?" Liz asked, tucking the towel back on the rack.

"Not quite. You see, I feel this – this presence. Like someone is touching me, or standing behind me. But whenever I turn—"

Knock-knock-knock.

The sharp rapping on the French windows interrupted Gabbie in mid-sentence. She spun quickly to look and saw a pale face pressed against the glass. "Oh, god!"

"It's just Colin," Liz said, moving to let him in. "Now try to calm down."

"Colin?" Gabbie's hand instantly flew to her hair that she hadn't combed. Then she looked down at her terry-cloth robe. It was comfortable, but definitely not something you would wear to greet a new boyfriend. "What's he doing here?" Gabbie whispered.

"I called him," Liz whispered back with a coy smile. "I thought you might want to see him."

"Yes, I do," Gabbie said, frantically smoothing her hair and trying to retie her robe. "But not looking like this."

"Too late. Can't turn back now." Liz flung open the door. "Hi, Colin, we were just talking about you."

Colin stepped in to the kitchen out of the rain. The tall, blond young man was dripping wet, his jeans and red windbreaker mottled with wet spots. He smiled apologetically at Gabbie. "I heard you shout. I didn't mean to scare you."

"You didn't scare me, Colin." Gabbie grabbed another kitchen towel and handed it to him. "I've just been a little jumpy lately."

"A little." Liz rolled her eyes.

Colin took the towel and quickly rubbed his hair and face with it. Then he took off his windbreaker. Underneath, his plaid flannel shirt was soaked. "Pardon my, uh – irregular appearance."

"Never mind," Gabbie said, giggling. She

tugged at the lapel of her robe. "Look at me – my oldest bathrobe."

"Want some hot chocolate?" Liz asked, wiping up the puddle of water on the floor, which was wet from Colin's running shoes.

"Thanks, Liz, but I can't stay long." He rubbed his hands together to get warm. "I had to beg my housemaster for a pass, and then bribe my roommate for a car. Mine's being fixed. Then the drive from Ridley took longer than usual because of this lousy rain. And to top it all off, I couldn't find a parking place within a half-mile of Smith Hall."

"Come and sit down," Gabbie said. "At least until you get dry." She smiled at him warmly. "I'm really glad to see you."

"I wanted to see you before," Colin explained. "Did Liz tell you I wanted to come to the funeral?"

"I'm so glad you didn't," Gabbie said quickly. "It was a terrible experience."

He gave her a sympathetic smile. "I'm sure it was." He put one hand on hers and asked, gently, "So how are you doing, Bradford?"

"The truth?" Gabbie looked sideways, "Not that great."

"All she needs is a little TLC," Liz explained as she cleared the two mugs and saucers from the table. She pointed to the clock above the stove. "Which reminds me. Mrs Carruthers is going to be down here any second for bed check. It's ten o'clock."

"But Colin only just got here," Gabbie protested. "Maybe she'll let him stay for a few minutes, considering the circumstances."

"I'll sit on the front hall stairs and stand guard for a little bit," Liz said as she quickly washed and dried the mugs. "But whisper. Carruthers has canine ears."

"You're the best, Liz," Gabbie said gratefully.

"Yeah. Thanks, Red," Colin whispered.

"Be good." Liz wiggled her eyebrows at them as she left the kitchen. "And if you can't be good, at least be quiet."

Once they were alone, Gabbie felt awkward and shy. She and Colin had only been dating for a month, which meant that they'd gone to one dance, a few movies and out to dinner. They were still pretty casual. She didn't want the awfulness of the past few days to affect their relationship.

"You look wasted," Colin told her, truthfully. He squeezed her hand. "But beautiful."

"It was a rough day," she admitted. Gabbie tried not to let her voice crack. "I spent the morning talking to an FBI agent and the afternoon at the funeral."

"Was the agent's name Scharfe?" Colin asked.

"Yes." Gabbie blinked in surprise. "Ron Scharfe. But how did you know?"

Colin looked at the floor, embarrassed. "He talked to me yesterday afternoon. On the phone."

"I don't believe this!" Gabbie let go of his hand and paced to the sink. "Why would he call you? What did he want?"

"He asked me questions about you. About us. How long we've been together. He wanted to know what you said about your parents." Colin peered at Gabbie through a lock of his blond hair. "I told him you hardly talked to me at all about them."

Gabbie winced, covering her face with her hands. "I can't believe he'd drag you in to this."

"Hey, it's OK." Colin moved to stand in front of Gabbie, unsure of how to comfort her.

"I just hope I didn't say anything stupid. My dad says if he calls again I shouldn't say anything. He's checking this out with his lawyer."

"Oh, great!" Gabbie threw her hands in the air. "Now your father is involved. I *hate* this!"

Colin touched her cheek. "Try not to let it get to you. I guess he's just doing his job."

"But why doesn't he go and talk to someone else?" Gabbie complained. "Like people from my father's office. He's acting like I had something to do with their deaths."

"Well, that's just plain stupid. No one would believe it for a second. The guy's grasping at straws because he doesn't have a real suspect." Colin's voice was growing louder and more passionate.

Gabbie put her finger to her lips. "Shh." She couldn't help smiling. "But thanks for the vote of confidence."

"Well, the whole idea is absurd," Colin continued in a whisper. "I mean, you were right here at White Springs when the murder happened. And Prescott is an hour and a half from here."

"Actually, I was in the library late, Colin. No

one else was there. It doesn't look good as an alibi."

Colin shrugged. "What about the librarian?"

"She must have been in the office, or shelving books. No one was at the front desk when I left." For the first time since her parents' death, Gabbie thought specifically about her actions that night.

"Someone must have seen you." Colin's tone of voice sounded a little less confident than before. "I mean, after all, you were here. And the murder was there. Right?"

Gabbie rubbed her temples with one hand. "Right." This was not how she had wanted her reunion with Colin to turn out. She had hoped that they'd just pick up where they'd left off, and forget about all the terribleness that had happened to her.

Liz poked her head round the corner. "Better go, Colin. Carruthers is doing her bed check!"

Colin leaned forward and gave Gabbie a quick kiss on the lips. "I just want you to know that I'm here for you if you need me, Bradford." He paused and looked at her. "You believe me, don't you?"

"Yes." Gabbie nodded her head. "I believe you."

"I'll call you." Then he grabbed his sopping wet windbreaker from the back of the kitchen chair, opened the French windows, and disappeared in to the rain.

The moment the door clicked shut, Gabbie got that feeling again – the unshakable sensation that someone was in the room with her. She spun round to look at the chair where she'd seen the figure earlier.

Nothing. No one was there.

"Get a grip, Gabbie," she murmured to herself.

Gabbie stood for a time in the silent kitchen. Then, taking a deep breath, she walked over and snapped off the kitchen light.

In the darkness, she felt the unmistakable pressure of a very cold hand covering her own.

CHAPTER SEVEN

Uranus is joined with Saturn, making you doubly cautious in nature. That's good, because the unexpected awaits you somewhere today and it would be wise to err on the side of caution. Stay close to home.

Bells woke Gabbie on Sunday morning. The constant, dull *bong, bong, bong* that called the academy's girls to chapel. Gabbie pulled her pillow over her head. *If I never set foot in a church again, it will be too soon.*

From her position under the pillow, she could just make out the numbers on the digital clock by her bedside. Eleven in the morning. The scare in the kitchen the night before had given her yet another sleepless night. It wasn't until dawn that she had finally been able to close her eyes and rest.

"I'm beginning to feel like a vampire,"

Gabbie muttered with her cheek pressed against the sheet. "Sleeping only in the day, and staying awake all night."

Bong bong bong.

"Oh, stop your clanging!" Gabbie shouted, wrapping the pillow tighter round her head.

"It's Oscar the Grouch," Liz called from across the room. "Helping us greet the day."

Gabbie lifted one corner of her pillow and peered at her friend. "I'm sorry, Liz, but I had a terrible night."

Liz was already dressed for church in a pink linen skirt and white blouse with pearls. It was a requirement that White Springs girls attend chapel at least twice a month. Liz always waited for the last two weeks to put in her required time.

"Don't wait for me," Gabbie murmured. "I just can't make it."

Liz stuffed her purse with her crossword puzzle book, gum and the horoscope section from the Sunday paper. "Since you won't be there to dish the dirt with me, I'll just take along a few items for entertainment."

"Hey, don't take the horoscope!" Gabbie protested. "I was looking forward to reading it."

"Then I'll just take a glance at it before I go." Liz pulled the horoscope page out of her purse and scanned it quickly. A dark frown formed on her face.

"What?" Gabbie was starting to be really awake. "Tell me. What is it?"

Liz shoved it back in her purse. "You don't want to know. It basically says today is a good day for staying in. It looks like that applies to all the signs."

Gabbie sat up in bed, clutching Edward her trusty bear, to her chest. "Not fair. That's worse than letting me read it."

Liz checked her watch. "Look, I'll let you see it after chapel. OK? I have to hurry to get a back-row seat."

The back pews always filled up first. Latecomers were forced to take a pew at the front, which meant they had to look as if they were paying attention to the service.

Liz bolted for the door, but as she reached it, she snapped her fingers. "Almost forgot." She backed up two steps and grabbed a folded piece of paper from her desk. "Found this shoved under our door this morning. It has your name on it."

Liz hurled the letter like a Frisbee towards Gabbie. Naturally it missed the bed completely, landing on the carpet.

"Thanks for nothing," Gabbie called, throwing the covers back and slowly getting out of bed. It seemed like every joint in her body ached from tension. She put a hand to her lower back and stretched. Major tension. Then she bent over to pick up the letter.

The handwriting was spidery, almost childish. Gabbie didn't recognize it. But what she did recognize was that chill. The same one she'd felt in the pink bedroom at her parents' house. Gabbie unfolded the note.

YOU'RE GOING TO PAY
FOR WHAT YOU DID.

Gabbie stared at the piece of paper for several moments. Then she dropped it on the floor by the bed.

Feet pounded on the carpeted floor behind her. "Gabbie, what's the matter?" Darby asked. She was half-dressed for church in a black mini skirt and leather waistcoat. A cigarette hung out of her mouth. Tiffany Randell, still in her slip and holding a hairbrush, was right behind her.

"What do you mean?" Gabbie asked hoarsely.

"You screamed," Tiffany told her. "It sounded like a wild animal."

"I screamed?" Gabbie blinked at her surroundings. "How could I have screamed?"

Darby spotted the piece of paper at Gabbie's feet and picked it up. She read it quickly. "*Sacré bleu*! What does this mean, Gabbie?" she asked.

"I'm not sure," Gabbie said, slumping on to the side of her twin bed.

Tiffany, who had read the note over Darby's shoulder, drawled, "Maybe someone thinks you had something to do with your parents' murder."

"No way!" Darby blew a puff of smoke at Tiffany. "Tiffany, your hair spray has poisoned your brain."

"Ooh, stop that!" Tiffany coughed and fanned at the air with her brush. "What else could it mean?"

Gabbie caught sight of her reflection in the mirror on the chest of drawers. Her face had lost all its colour and her hair was matted. *I really do look like a vampire.* She rubbed her cheeks, trying to get some colour in them. Then she made herself focus on Tiffany. "I was right here the night my parents were killed. You know that."

"How would I know that?" Tiffany bent her head over from the waist and combed her hair from the hairline to the tips of her blonde hair. "I went to the movies that night, and I didn't see you when I got back." She flipped her head back up and her hair fluffed beautifully on to her shoulders.

Gabbie turned to Darby, who was searching for her ashtray. "Darby, you know I was here."

"I'm not sure. Where was I on Wednesday night?" Darby murmured as she searched blindly under her bed with one arm. "Let's see. Justin? Peter? No, actually, that was the night I had that horrible headache." She held up the ashtray she'd found under the bed. "I took a sleeping pill I swiped from my mother and slept until morning."

"You shouldn't take other people's medication," Tiffany scolded.

"Thank you, doctor," Darby said, stubbing the remains of her cigarette out in the tin.

"So where were you exactly?" Tiffany said, pointing her hairbrush at Gabbie.

"I was in the library, studying," Gabbie said with a shrug.

Tiffany raised one eyebrow. "But the library closes at nine-thirty."

"I checked out a video on birds for my biology report," Gabbie explained as she stroked Edward the bear's nearly furless head. "When I got back from the library, I watched the video in the TV room."

"Odd I didn't hear it," Tiffany said, folding her arms across her chest and cocking her head. "I mean, my room is right above the TV room. I usually hear everything."

"I kept the volume low so I wouldn't disturb anyone," Gabbie snapped back impatiently. She was starting to get really irritated with Tiffany's questions.

"But I didn't hear you come upstairs to bed, Gabbie, and you know what a light sleeper I am," Tiffany persisted.

Gabbie got up from her bed and moved to her wardrobe to get her robe. "I fell asleep in the TV room, and then I came up here late – about two o'clock."

Tiffany looked skeptical. "Funny Carruthers didn't find you during bed check."

"I was probably in the bathroom," Gabbie blurted out in exasperation. Tiffany's relentless skepticism was starting to make Gabbie feel like she was making the whole thing up.

"Give it a rest, Tiffany," Darby said, stepping between the two girls. "What are you, anyway? The FBI?"

"No, but I plan to be an attorney someday." She flashed her white toothy smile at Darby. "I'm just honing my interrogation skills."

"Well, hone them on somebody else," Darby said. "Gabbie's going through a rough time – remember?"

"Sorry, Gabbie." Tiffany flipped her hair off her shoulders. "I didn't mean anything by it."

Brrring.

The phone on the wall broke the tension. "I'll get it!" Gabbie made a dive for it, glad for the interruption. But the second she picked up the receiver a penetrating chill, like opening a freezer door, washed over her.

"Hello? Hello?"

All Gabbie heard on the line was the sound of barely audible breathing.

"What do you want?" Gabbie demanded, in a less than firm voice. She was trying hard to squelch the fear bubbling inside her. "Answer me!"

"Who is it?" Darby called from across the room.

Gabbie slammed down the receiver. "Crank call."

"*Mon Dieu*!" Darby shook her head and moved to the mirror. "The guys are at it again." She took a lip-liner pencil out of her make-up basket and drew a sharp magenta line round her mouth. "Every few weeks they start another ridiculous round of obscene calls. What was it this time – a heavy breather?"

Gabbie shrugged her shoulders and stared at the phone. "Not really. Actually, just the opposite."

"Well, I would just love to chat with you two about obscene phone calls," Tiffany said, "but I need to get dressed."

"So who's stopping you?" Darby asked, gesturing to the door.

Tiffany made a move to exit, but her way was blocked by an underclassman holding a square white envelope with the White Springs Academy seal on the outside.

"Mrs Albion sent me with this note." The girl handed the note to Gabbie and then hurried away, intimidated by the mere presence of the older girls.

"Maybe it's news of some late-breaking clues," Tiffany said, hanging round to see what the envelope held.

Gabbie hesitantly opened the envelope and announced with mixed feelings, "Mrs Albion has invited me to brunch."

"*C'est si bon!*" Darby threw her arms in the air. "It must be your math scores. Or your newspaper articles."

Having a meal with Mrs Albion usually meant that you had accomplished something wonderful – topped the honour roll, or performed some outstanding community service.

"You get to have one of those formal, old-fashioned meals with finger bowls and fruit ices between the courses," Darby said. "Or so I've heard. I've never been invited."

"That's because you have too many holes in your earlobes," Tiffany said with disgust.

"Better than having too many holes in your brain," Darby shot back.

Another day, Gabbie would have laughed at Darby and Tiffany's sparring. It was all part of their daily life at school. But today she only felt dread. What could Mrs Albion want? Why was she being summoned?

Gabbie returned to her wardrobe, in search of a suitable outfit to wear to her luncheon with the headmistress. Then she took a shower to try to make the dark circles that were becoming permanent fixtures under her eyes disappear. An hour later she left for brunch with a sinking feeling in her stomach.

Mrs Albion was her usual smiling, genteel self. The dining room was pleasant, with fresh flowers and china. Mrs Albion's cook set course after course in front of Gabbie. But all she could do was pick at the food and wait for Mrs Albion to "get down to business".

Finally the meal was over, and Mrs Albion steered Gabbie in to the formal living room. Gabbie perched on an antique tapestry love seat across from the headmistress.

"Gabrielle, dear. I know you're going through a difficult time. But we have to have a very serious talk." Mrs Albion smiled over her glasses, like she always did. But this smile seemed tight. "I've been speaking on the phone with your father's lawyer. And you're in a bit of an odd position, dear."

Here it comes, Gabbie thought. *They want me to leave White Springs.*

"Of course there's much to sort out, Gabrielle," Mrs Albion continued, "but first and foremost is the matter of your custody."

"Custody?" Gabbie's heart thudded in her chest. *They're going to force me to live with Aunt Louise!*

"Obviously, your aunt is the logical choice. But she has declined." Mrs Albion pursed her lips. "She feels she's not up to raising a teenager at this point in her life."

Gabbie wanted to shout with joy. Anyone would be better than Aunt Louise.

"I've also been talking to a Mr Scharfe," Mrs Albion went on. "He is the agent handling the investigation of your parents' deaths."

"Yes, I know," Gabbie said.

"It appears that we are to become your – caretakers. At least until a few things can be straightened out."

"White Springs Academy?" Gabbie was confused. "But what does that mean? The academy has always been my caretaker."

"This would be different, Gabrielle." Mrs Albion stared at her hands in her lap, choosing her words carefully. "Mr Scharfe has asked that we confine you to campus."

"What?" Gabbie rose to her feet.

"And if you need to leave the grounds, he has asked that a chaperone go with you."

"You mean I'm a prisoner?" Gabbie's voice was quivering.

Mrs Albion gestured for Gabbie to sit down again. Her voice was painstakingly calm. "In a highly publicized murder case like this, every possibility must be carefully investigated. There are procedures, dear. And they take time."

Gabbie was too agitated to sit down. She paced the living room, sputtering, "But how could anyone think I murdered my own parents? Their house is an hour and a half from here. I went to class that day. I went to the library—"

"Unfortunately no one saw you that night," Mrs Albion interrupted. "Not at the library, or at Smith Hall. And to add to the problem, you borrowed Elizabeth Sutton's car for at least part of that evening."

Gabbie's jaw dropped. "Did Liz tell you that?"

"Agent Scharfe has been talking to everyone."

Gabbie took a deep breath, trying to stay

calm. "Yes, I borrowed her car," she admitted, "to go into town for some shampoo. But that's it. I came right back and went to the library."

"When did you return the keys?" asked Mrs Albion.

"I put them on Liz's chest of drawers that night, before I went to bed."

Mrs Albion took a sip of the glass of water she had brought into the living room and Gabbie noticed her hand was quivering. "I know this is a horrible situation, dear, but you must look at it from the investigator's point of view." She set the glass on its coaster. "You did have the means to go to your parents' house. And no one saw you from round six o'clock that night until the next morning."

Gabbie's eyes widened in horror. *She doesn't believe me.*

"But why would I murder my parents?" Gabbie asked. "I never saw them. You know that." Her throat ached as tears sprang to her eyes. "I accepted a long time ago that they weren't a part of my life."

Mrs Albion went to Gabbie and put an arm round her. "I know, Gabrielle. I do understand. I've helped raise you – as though you were my own daughter. You've grown to be a fine young woman, considering the hand you've been dealt."

Gabbie's tears were now coming fast and furious as she tried to choke out a response to Mrs Albion's words.

Mrs Albion produced a handkerchief from the sleeve of her sweater and handed it to Gabbie. "You will have to be very strong, Gabrielle. There will probably be a lot more unpleasantness before this investigation is over."

"I'll try," was all Gabbie could manage to choke out.

"Good." Mrs Albion patted Gabbie's arm. "Now, how about some chocolate torte? Cook made your favourite dessert."

Gabbie blinked at Mrs Albion in amazement. *She wants me to eat chocolate and pretend it's all better. I can't.*

"I'm sorry, Mrs Albion," Gabbie said, trying to regain her composure. "But I need to be by myself for a while."

Gabbie felt like an automaton, standing and smiling politely. Shaking hands with Mrs Albion. Thanking her for the lovely meal.

Crossing the grass to Smith Hall, Gabbie

realized she was truly alone. No one, not even Liz, could help her avoid what was happening. As she passed the ivy-covered buildings of the academy that had once seemed like an oasis of calm to her, she also knew that now there was nowhere to hide.

Gabbie crossed through the empty living room of Smith Hall and plodded up the stairs to the first floor. She could vaguely make out the sounds of a movie being shown in the TV room, but other than that, the dorm seemed deserted.

The door to Gabbie's room was closed. She reached for her key that she wore on a chain round her neck. As she moved to unlock her room, she noticed a slip of paper on the floor. The same stationery as before.

Gabbie picked it up and unfolded the paper.

IT SHOULD HAVE BEEN YOU.
NEXT TIME IT WILL BE.

CHAPTER EIGHT

Mercury has hold of you like a puppy with a slipper. Normally talkative, you are afraid you'll say the wrong thing. Someone else is talking too much and that makes you wary. Whether they are telling you lies, or telling others lies about you, keep your mind open – and your mouth shut.

The phone in Gabbie's dorm room rang loudly. Both she and Liz jumped at the sound. It was Wednesday afternoon and they'd been studying quietly for nearly two hours, with only the sound of the ticking clock and the steady rain against the window.

Gabbie instinctively picked it up. "Hello?"

No one was there. Again.

She hung up the phone and shouted, "I hate this!"

"What?" Liz closed her math book and

turned in her chair to face Gabbie. The two of them were wearing their usual study uniforms – comfortable old jeans and torn T-shirts.

"This is the fifth call I've had like that in the last two days!"

Liz waved it off. "It's just some guys being idiots. It happens to everyone."

"But it doesn't," Gabbie pointed out. "It only happens when I answer."

"Coincidence. It's nothing to worry about." Liz stood up and stretched her arms above her head. "Do you want to take a break and get something to drink? This calculus is numbing my brain."

"I want to show you something first." Gabbie reached under her bed where she kept a shoe box full of letters and newspaper clippings. She removed the two notes she'd received and gave them to Liz.

Liz looked them over and let out a shocked gasp. "When did you get these?"

"Sunday, when the calls began."

Liz folded the notes and handed them back to Gabbie. "I think you should tell Mrs Carruthers or Mrs Albion. Even if this is just a practical joke, it's pretty sick, and they would want to know."

Gabbie moved to look out of the window at the endless rain. "I'm afraid to tell anyone besides you."

"Why?" asked Liz.

"After all the mean things that have been printed in the newspapers about me, I don't know who to trust." She pointed to the box of clippings. "Look at them. Look what people are saying about me."

Liz spread the clippings out on the bed. They were from *The Washington Post* and the *Richmond News-Leader*. There was even an obituary from the *New York Times*. "Where'd you get all these?"

"From Tiffany – who else? She pretends she's doing me a favour by cutting them out. 'I thought you'd like to know,' she tells me. But I swear she's enjoying this."

Liz wrinkled her nose. "Tiffany looks like a princess but she's really just a toad."

"Read this one." Gabbie pointed to an article from the *Baltimore Sun*. It contained a paragraph describing an "incident" in which "the ambassador's only daughter screamed at Louise Palmer, sister of the deceased Mrs Bradford, and refused to accompany the family party to the cemetery."

Liz rolled her eyes. "So you acted weird at your parents' funeral. Big deal. How were you supposed to act? Calm and happy?"

"It probably wouldn't have seemed so strange if it weren't for the terrible things my aunt told the reporter." Gabbie shuffled through the clippings for the rest of the article and read it out loud. "Gabrielle has always been a self-centred child. I don't recall her ever showing any affection for her parents."

Liz shook her head. "I think some people are just born evil. What's her sign?"

"The snake," Gabbie muttered. "But it's not just Aunt Louise. Look at this article. It's an interview with a woman named Vera Kauffman, who was supposedly my mother's best friend."

Liz looked over Gabbie's shoulder and read, "The Bradfords could never get their daughter to visit them. Not when they were in Africa, nor during Nick's posting in Southeast Asia. Even after Nick and Susan moved back to DC, their daughter never made an appearance. She broke her mother's heart."

"I never met that woman," Gabbie said, crumpling the article into a tiny ball and hurling it at the wall. "I never even heard my mother mention her name, and yet she says these things about me to the newspaper."

"People will say anything just to get their name in the paper," Liz said. "Try not to let it hurt you, Gabbie."

Gabbie scooped all the clippings together and shoved them back in the box. Her eyes were burning from tears that threatened to come. "But why hasn't anyone interviewed me? I'd love to tell the newspapers about my warm, caring parents. I could even show them the letters lovingly inscribed—" Gabbie pretended to write in the air. "Dear Gabrielle. I'm so sorry, but a visit this Christmas would be inconvenient for us. We will be in Paris with friends. Maybe spring break. Mother."

Liz wrapped her arm round Gabbie's shoulder. "Oh, Gabbie, don't think about it. That's all in the past. They can't hurt you any more."

"No, they can't hurt me." Gabbie slammed the lid back on the shoe box and threw it under the bed. "But their friends sure can."

"Only if you let them." Liz put her hands on her hips and ordered, "Number one, don't read the clippings. Two, tell Tiffany to shove it.

Better yet, I'll tell her myself. It would give me great pleasure."

Gabbie grabbed Edward and curled up on her bed. "Maybe I deserve this."

"*What*!" Liz threw a quilted pillow at Gabbie. "Don't even talk like that."

Gabbie stroked the top of her stuffed bear's nearly threadbare head. "Maybe I am bad. Evil."

"No!" Liz responded.

Gabbie cocked her head. "My parents must have thought so. Otherwise they wouldn't have sent me away."

Liz was getting impatient. "That's not true, and you know it! Your dad was assigned to some new political trouble spot every other year. They wanted you to have some stability."

"No. I'm quite certain that my parents just didn't like me."

"Gabbie—"

"Look at the difference between our parents," Gabbie cut in.

"How do you mean?"

"Well, your mom and dad obviously love you. They adore you. They have nicknames for you, they call you all the time."

"We have arguments all the time, too," Liz cut in.

"But then you kiss and make up. Right?"

"Right," Liz admitted.

"Well," Gabbie swallowed hard. "I've never told anybody this before." She stared down at her bear. "My mother never touched me. Ever. At the end of any visit, my father would force himself to hug me goodbye. But my mother always had an excuse not to touch me. She'd be holding packages in her arms, or she'd already be sitting in the car, or she'd be coming down with a cold. Something."

"You're just imagining that, Gabbie."

Gabbie leaped to her feet. "Don't ever say that to me!" she shouted fiercely. "I mean it."

Liz was so startled she stumbled backwards in to her desk chair. "I'm sorry, Gabbie. I'm only trying to help."

Gabbie was immediately full of remorse at her outburst. "I'm sorry, Liz. It's just that I've lived with their – their hatred my entire life." Gabbie moved to the full-length mirror by Liz's desk and leaned with her head resting against her reflection. "I've run out of excuses to make for them."

Liz came up beside Gabbie and quietly took her hand. "Gabbie, do you think you could talk to the school therapist? She might be able help you get through this, because. . ." Her voice caught in her throat slightly. "Because I really don't know what to say or do."

"Maybe I should." Gabbie squeezed Liz's hand. She lifted her head and examined her reflection. "Do you think people are born good or bad?"

"I think we're all a little of both," Liz said, smoothing Gabbie's hair away from her face and smiling into the mirror. "Especially you!"

"Me? Why me?"

"Because you're a Gemini," Liz explained. "The good twin and the bad twin. One minute you're the life of the party and the next you need time to yourself. The good news is that, although you may get a bit melodramatic at times, no Gemini mood is permanent."

"Melodramatic!" Gabbie repeated indignantly. "Me?"

The door suddenly swept open, banging against the wall. Darby had only caught the last two words of their exchange but she immediately jumped into their conversation. "You are the most melodramatic person in Smith Hall."

"I am not," denied Gabbie.

Darby retrieved her pack of cigarettes from under her pillow and pulled out her tin from beneath the bed. "What about The Mouse That Ate Smith Hall?" she kidded, lighting her cigarette with a disposable lighter she pulled from the pocket of her jeans.

"Not that old story!" Gabbie covered her face with her hands and groaned. "That was two years ago."

"You ran out into the hall screaming at the top of your voice that some hideous monster had taken over our room," Liz chimed in.

"But that wasn't the end of it." Darby exhaled a big puff of blue smoke. "You ordered everyone to grab weapons and call the police."

"She wanted us to call out the National Guard," Liz giggled.

Darby swooped her arm in a big circle. "So everyone came running, with brooms, mops, kitchen knives and baseball bats – anything they could find to help you battle this beast."

Liz was clutching her stomach now, doubled over with laughter. "And then it turned out to be– "

"Rebecca Sweeney's pet white mouse!"

Darby and Liz shouted in unison.

Gabbie couldn't help it. Their laughter was infectious and she had to join in. It felt so good. The best she'd felt in a week. She wiped the tears – tears of laughter – from her cheeks and chuckled, "Boy, did I feel like an idiot."

Liz nodded. "Darby, remember the time Gabbie got a C on her biology test and went berserk?"

"Who could forget." Darby gestured to their room. "She destroyed this place. She was *completement fou*!"

"I only destroyed my part of the room," Gabbie protested. "And I didn't actually destroy it, I merely hurled a few books to the floor. But they were *my* books, and I picked them up almost immediately."

"Yeah, sure," Liz snorted. "You forget about the bowl of popcorn you overturned. I was picking little yellow kernels out of my clothes and sheets, and the rug, for weeks after."

Gabbie folded her arms across her chest and turned on Liz. "What about you, Miss Sagittarius? I've seen you after several horse shows when nobody wanted to be round you – not even your horse."

"Let's face it," Darby said, taking another deep drag from her forbidden cigarette. "None of us is perfect." Then she coughed hoarsely. "I really shouldn't do this – it's bad for my health."

"Besides the fact that you could get expelled," Liz pointed out. "And the rest of us could get black lung disease."

Brring!

The phone cut through their conversation like a bolt of lightning. Gabbie and Liz stared at each other.

"Should we answer it?" Liz whispered.

"No!" Gabbie cried. A cold feeling, like ice-water, spread down her spine. "Let someone else pick it up."

"Do you want me to answer it?" Darby asked, thinking this was another game.

Brring.

"Maybe it's my parents," Liz said. "They told me they were going to call this evening."

Brrring.

"It could be Colin," Gabbie said, staring mesmerized at the phone. "He said, if the rain ever stopped, he would call to set up a tennis date."

"Well, don't just stand there," Darby said, hastily stubbing out her cigarette in the tin "It could be for me."

Gabbie, who was nearest the phone, tentatively picked up the receiver. "Hello?" Her mouth felt dry and cottony.

"Hello," said a friendly girl's voice. "May I speak to Tiffany? This is Cassandra."

Gabbie put her hand to her chest and smiled with relief at Liz. It was a real call.

"Sure, just a minute," Gabbie said. She moved to the door dividing their room and Tiffany's. "Tiffany! It's Cassie on the phone."

Tiffany peered round the corner, her face covered in a mask of thick, mint-green paste. She had just begun her daily ritual of facial and manicure. "I'll take it in here," she said, shutting the door.

Gabbie waited for Tiffany to pick up the phone and, just before she did, a sinister voice rasped in Gabbie's ear:

"Fooled you!"

CHAPTER NINE

Mercury is at odds with Saturn, which could make you appear to be malicious or spiteful. Add to that the progressed Moon touching off that Saturn aspect and you are in danger of being betrayed by false friends. Top that with Saturn sitting in the 12th House, and you have secret sorrows, loss, and danger of accidents. You are maxed out over something. Back off. Regroup.

YOUR TIME IS NEARLY UP.
CAN YOU HEAR THE CLOCK TICKING?

Gabbie stared dully at the note she'd just found in her notebook. It was penned in the same spidery handwriting as the other two notes. She had just opened her textbook in Mr LeFarge's Thursday morning class on World Religions, and there it was.

Gabbie didn't scream. Somehow she'd known the note would be there. Just as she'd known when the phone would ring. It was the sudden cold, like wind off a glacier, that had warned her.

Now she held what was very clearly a death threat in the palm of her hand. At the front of the room, Mr LeFarge's voice droned on about the Hindu mandala, the great wheel of life. Something about reincarnation and karma, how spirits were destined to ride this wheel over and over in different lives and manifestations, in search of perfection.

Gabbie tried to take her mind off the note and concentrate on the lecture, but her head was pounding. A constant throbbing at her temples kept her from focusing on anything but the pain.

She reached in her book bag on the floor, feeling round for the bottle of aspirin she always carried. Her hand brushed against something soft and oddly shaped, and instantly she flinched. Upon realizing it wasn't a mouse or anything alive, Gabbie carefully reached back in the bag and pulled out the object. For a moment she had no idea what the brown furry thing could be. And then she recognized it.

"Ugggh!" she screamed, leaping to her feet. Everyone in class turned to stare at her. Mr LeFarge froze at the blackboard, his chalk held in mid-air.

What Gabbie held in her hand was the tattered arm from a stuffed animal. Edward the stuffed bear's missing arm. It had disappeared years ago. Now, suddenly, here it was in her book bag. But how could that be?

She hurled the arm at the floor. "Someone is deliberately trying to scare me!" Gabbie shrieked. "Well, I want you to stop!" She jerked from side to side, glaring at everyone she could. "If you have something to say to me, say it to my face. Just stop torturing me!"

Mr LeFarge set the chalk in its tray and crossed to Gabbie's desk. The class was dead silent. No one moved a muscle. They watched as the teacher carefully retrieved the teddy bear's severed arm. "I would like all of you to turn to page 272, and finish reading the section on the mandala," he told the class quietly. Then he gestured for Gabbie to follow him to a far corner of the room.

"I don't know what's going on, Gabrielle," he said, keeping his voice low. "But we can't have this kind of disruption. Not in my class."

"Someone is playing cruel jokes on me, Mr LeFarge!" Gabbie complained. She pointed to the tiny bear's arm. "And they know how to hurt me."

She started to explain about her bear, how its arm had been lost when she was a child, so long ago that even Gabbie didn't remember how it was lost. Her explanation must have been more jumbled than she thought because Mr LeFarge stopped her abruptly.

"I'm sorry, Gabbie, we can't talk about this now." He checked his watch. "I have a mere forty-five minutes left in which to explain the differences between Hinduism, Buddhism and Shintoism. Until we can meet with Mrs Albion and discuss this matter privately, I think it's best if you return to your room and stay there."

"Why?" Gabbie screeched. Her face was burning a bright red and she could feel small beads of perspiration dotting her hairline. "What have I done?"

"Nothing at all. I mean that." Mr LeFarge, who was one of the youngest teachers on campus and the object of numerous crushes, tried to appear sympathetic. "Gabbie, I know you're overwrought about your parents' death – and who could blame you?"

"I'm not overwrought about my parents, Mr LeFarge! I'm overwrought about Edward's missing arm showing up in my book bag after twelve years."

Mr LeFarge checked his watch again. "Look, I wish I could discuss your personal problems with you but I have a responsibility to the rest of the class. Now, please do as I say. Return to your room, and I'll have Mrs Albion call you."

Tears burning her eyes, Gabbie grabbed her book bag and stormed out of the classroom, slamming the door as hard as she could. The jamb was still rattling when she heard a familiar laugh behind her.

Gabbie spun to face the empty hallway, as a voice whispered, *"Got you!"*

Voices, and notes. Harassing her, threatening her, driving her out of her mind. It was all too much for Gabbie. She covered her ears and ran outside on to the commons. Then she ducked her head and raced as fast as her legs could carry her for Smith Hall. Blinded by her tears, she ploughed headlong into another student.

"Ow!" Gabbie clutched her head.

"Hey, Bradford! Slow down." Colin caught hold of her shoulders and said, "It's not good to run this early in the day."

Gabbie blinked at him for several seconds, unsure if she was imagining him or he was truly real.

"Colin?" she asked, touching his face. "What are you doing here?"

It was his turn to look confused. "You called and asked me to come. Remember?"

Gabbie didn't remember at all. "When did I call?"

"This morning." Colin studied her face. "You said you needed to see me. That it was very important."

Gabbie licked her lips. *I really am losing my mind.* "Things have been a little crazy for me," she explained slowly. "But I'm really happy to see you. I need someone sane in my life right now."

"That's me," Colin said, with a mock salute. "Mr Sane. At your service."

"Colin, listen," Gabbie said, barely smiling at his joke, "I have to get away from here. From the academy."

"But what about Agent Scharfe and—?"

Gabbie cut him off with the wave of a hand. "I don't care about the restrictions. If I don't get out of here now, I really think I'm going to lose it. Please."

"All right," Colin said with a shrug. "If that's what you want."

"It's what I need. Let me drop my books in my room, and I'll meet you in the parking lot by your car."

Colin gave her a thumbs-up sign and headed off. Gabbie ran the remaining distance to Smith Hall as fast as she could. After first checking to see if Mrs Carruthers was about, Gabbie tiptoed up to her room. As she approached her door, the familiar cold feeling spread down her spine again.

"Oh, god, no!"

Another white piece of paper was wedged beneath her door. Willing her hands to stop shaking, Gabbie unfolded it.

YOU'LL BE SORRY!

Without stopping to think, Gabbie unlocked her door and grabbed a jacket. She also grabbed the box of notes hidden under her bed, and added this latest threat to her collection. She had to show Colin.

When they arrived at the Coffee Beanery, Colin and Gabbie picked a cosy booth in the corner, away from the window. And away from nosy townspeople who might wonder what the two students, easily identifiable in their school clothes, were doing away from school in the middle of a Thursday morning.

"So what's in the box?" Colin asked after their breakfast was served. He was attacking a heaped plate of pancakes with blueberry syrup.

Gabbie sipped her iced coffee. "Are you sure you're ready for this?"

"Sure," he told her. "Let me have it."

Gabbie spread the notes out on the table and watched Colin's face harden while he read them. He let out a long, low whistle. "My God, Gabbie. Who's doing this?"

"I wish I knew. And today someone put the missing arm of my old stuffed bear in my book bag sometime before World Religions. It totally freaked me out."

Colin took a pen out of his pocket and grabbed some napkins. "Let's make a list of possible suspects. Anyone who comes into your head."

She took another sip of her coffee. "It has to be someone who knows me really well."

"OK," he said. "What about Tiffany? She rooms next to you, but I wouldn't call her a close friend."

"True," Gabbie narrowed her eyes. "And she seems obsessed with collecting newspaper clippings about my parents' murder."

Colin wrote Tiffany's name at the top of the list. "Who else?"

"Not Liz or Darby," Gabbie said firmly. "No way."

"Think, Bradford," Colin encouraged her. "How about someone in your classes? If not this year, last year."

"Well. . . there's Kirsten Pentz. A sophomore in my phys. ed. class last semester. She was mad at me because I didn't choose her for field hockey when I was captain."

"Is she still mad?" asked Colin.

"I'm not sure. She may have a possible grudge, but I—"

Colin added Kirsten's name to the list. "Hey, what about that girl you tutor?"

"Carrie?"

"Yeah. Don't you think she's a little weird? She's always bringing you gifts and phoning you."

Gabbie shook her head. "No. She's just really young and really lonely."

And she reminds me of me when I was her age.

"The only person who really truly hates me is my Aunt Louise," Gabbie said, taking a final drink of her coffee. "But she's not here. She's gone back to Florida or wherever it is she lives."

Colin examined the four notes again. "Official school stationery. Anyone could get that. Black ink. Everyone uses black ink."

"But look at the handwriting," Gabbie said. "Shaky and childish. Is someone trying to disguise their writing? But if they are, why not use a typewriter or computer? Just about everyone at White Springs has a PC."

"So tell me again how you discovered the notes," Colin said.

Gabbie explained that Liz had found the first note but the rest were either pushed under her door, or in her notebook, which meant that whoever wrote them had access to her room.

"So what do we know?" Colin murmured. "That this person has strange handwriting, can get into your room, knows you well—"

"And is a girl," Gabbie finished.

"How do we know that?" Colin asked.

"The phone calls."

"Calls?" Colin blinked in amazement. "You've been getting calls too? Geez, Gabbie, why haven't you told campus security?"

"I'm afraid they won't believe me. I mean, no one else has heard her voice, except me."

"Next time, have Liz or Darby listen on the other line."

"Oh, she's too clever for that. She only talks to me." Gabbie bent her head forward and whispered. "And here's the really weird thing – I always know when it's her call. I get this really cold feeling just before I pick up the phone. Same with the notes. Somehow, *I know* they're going to be there."

Colin grew very quiet. He pushed his food away and stared at the napkin covered with his scribbled notes.

"What's the matter?" Gabbie asked, ducking her head to get a look at his face.

"I'm really worried about you," Colin finally said. "Maybe the pressure's getting too much for you."

"What are you saying?"

He looked into her eyes and his expression was troubled. "You've been under a lot of stress." Colin picked his words carefully. "Stress can make people do and say strange things."

"You think what's happening to me is caused by stress?"

"Obviously," a female voice from the next booth answered. "You've lost your mind, and are making all of this up."

"Shut up!" Gabbie snapped. "What do you know about anything?"

Colin turned white. "Don't shout at me, Gabbie."

Gabbie inhaled sharply. "I wasn't talking to you, Colin. I was talking to her."

"Who?"

"That girl in the next booth. Didn't you hear her? She said I was making all of this up."

Colin shook his head slowly. "No one said anything, Gabbie. Except you."

She spun round. The booth behind her was empty. So was the entire cafe, except for three old men sitting by the window smoking cigarettes.

"Somebody was there!" Gabbie insisted.

"I'll find her!" She ran to the door of the cafe, and out to the sidewalk.

Colin joined her outside, carrying her jacket and the box of notes. He grabbed her by the elbow to stop her from running up the street. "Stop it, Gabbie! Now listen to me. You're holding too much stuff inside. And I think maybe you're starting to crack from the strain."

Gabbie shrugged out of his grasp. "Everyone thinks I'm losing my grip. Well, maybe there's a good reason for it."

"Gabbie— "

"Try having your parents murdered, and everyone on the planet suspect you. Then try getting a few calls and notes threatening your life." Gabbie's head was throbbing and a blinding fury was building inside her. "Maybe you'd start to crack, too."

Colin tried to keep his voice calm. "I'm not criticizing you. I just think you should get some help – talk to someone, that's all."

"Talk? *Talk*?"

Suddenly all Gabbie wanted to do was lash out. To hurt somebody. Anybody. A roaring noise, like radio static, rose up in her ears, drowning out her scream of anger and frustration.

The next thing Gabbie knew, she was sitting on a park bench beside Colin's car. She was breathing heavily, in short, tight gasps. The windshield of his red Mazda had been smashed into a pattern that looked like a giant spider's web.

What happened? What am I doing here? What's this heavy weight in my hand? Gabbie looked down. She was holding a large, rough brick.

"Get in the car."

Colin was standing over her. Gabbie looked up and flinched at the look in his eyes. She had never seen such an expression of anger, revulsion and hurt, all mixed into one.

Gabbie was afraid to speak. "Did I. . . ?"

"I don't want to talk about it," he snapped.

Numb with shock, Gabbie set the heavy brick on the ground and mechanically got in the car. *What have I done?*

Colin said nothing. He started the engine and immediately turned on the car radio. He didn't speak a word to her the entire way back to White Springs Academy.

In the parking lot, he stopped but didn't turn off the engine. He looked straight ahead while

Gabbie gathered her belongings and got out of the car. She leaned down to the open window. "Colin, please. I don't know what happened, but—"

He slammed the Mazda in gear and sped off before she could finish her sentence.

"I didn't do that, Mommy."

"Yes, she did. It's her fault."

"Not fair. I always get blamed."

Gabbie covered her ears and sank down on the ground. "Oh, god, what's happening to me?"

CHAPTER TEN

Gabbie could hear someone screaming. Screaming with rage. Screaming on and on. But who was it? Her head felt thick and clouded, as though she was trying to surface from a deep sleep.

"Why are you doing this to me?" the voice screeched. "I want you to stop it! Leave me alone."

Another voice broke through the fog in Gabbie's head. A pleading voice. "Gabbie! Gabbie, stop it!"

With a start, Gabbie snapped back into reality. Bright light streamed through the large room. All round her were girls in White Springs uniforms. The overpowering smell of meat-loaf and overcooked vegetables almost made her retch.

I'm in the cafeteria. What am I doing here?

Someone was whimpering nearby. Gabbie

turned. It was Tiffany.

Tiffany's face was pale and full of fear. Tears streaked her cheeks. Gabbie had never seen her look so bad.

Someone was tugging her arm. It was Liz. "Have you lost your mind?" she hissed, pulling Gabbie out of the cafeteria into the empty corridor. "Marching in here and accusing Tiffany of sending you death threats – in front of everyone!"

"No! I couldn't have!" Gabbie replied. "I don't remember doing that!"

Liz shook her head in disappointment. "Oh, Gabbie."

Not you, Liz. Not you, too. Even her closest friend, and strongest ally, didn't believe her. It was too much for Gabbie to bear. She ran from the cafeteria, searching for some place, any place, to hide. But her chest burned, and her breathing became shallower and shallower until she finally had to stop. She leaned against a black wrought-iron fence, clutching her chest. *Breathe!* The panic would not subside. It just kept growing within her, expanding uncontrollably like a cancer.

A soccer ball landed at Gabbie's feet with a

dull thud. She looked out through the fence to the playing fields where a group of middle school girls were waving at her. Gabbie tried to smile and wave. She picked up the ball, ready to toss it back.

But suddenly the dizziness came upon her again. And the paralyzing cold. It overcame Gabbie with such force that she could hardly stay on her feet. She gripped the fence, trying not to fall.

Then, as quickly as it came, the vertigo and cold left her. Gabbie looked round. She was still clinging to the fence. Someone was yelling, and several of the girls were in tears, pointing at her.

"Don't worry," Gabbie cried. "I'm going to throw your ball back. Here!"

But the ball wasn't in her hands any more. Where was it?

"Oh, my god!" Gabbie saw the ball impaled on one of the spikes of the fence. No one else was near. She had to have done it.

Gabbie stumbled away, frantic. *I need help. Desperately.*

She managed to make it to the phone booth next to the refreshment stand at the bottom of the bleachers. She fumbled in the pocket of her skirt for change, intending to call the school therapist. But when she reached for the door, something blocked her way.

A spectral image hovered in the air in front of her. It was the same one she had seen at the funeral and in the kitchen her first night back at Smith Hall. A dark-haired little girl, in a delicate white dress with lace trim at the collar and shoulders. Her large brown eyes glittered with malevolence.

"It won't do you any good to call. They'll never believe you."

"Who are you?" Gabbie demanded of the ghostly image.

"No one ever believed you."

The dark-haired little girl shimmered for a moment in the warm sunshine, then disappeared.

Gabbie's knees felt weak. She spun round, looking for someone to help her. The only person in her vicinity was a tall man in a rumpled blue suit. Agent Scharfe!

He was leaning against the fence where she had stood only moments earlier. The younger girls were gone but the punctured soccer ball was still impaled on the fence spike. The FBI agent was examining the ball and writing notes in his book. To Gabbie's horror, he picked up his camera and took a photo of the fence and the ball.

Evidence. More evidence about me.

Gabbie cautiously slipped away from the phone booth, trying not to let him see her. She decided to take the long way back to Smith Hall, along the heavily wooded footpath bordering the campus.

Gabbie's head ached. She couldn't remember when her thoughts and actions had been her own. When she hadn't heard voices or seen ghostly apparitions.

Maybe it's this place. White Springs was filled with too many reminders of her sad past. If she could just run away. Somewhere she'd never been before. Then maybe her head would clear. And the awful headaches would stop.

To Gabbie's dismay, Mrs Carruthers was on the porch of Smith Hall, watering the flowers. And, to make things worse, she spotted Gabbie and waved.

Does she know? Has someone told her about the cafeteria and the soccer ball? Is she waiting for me?

Realizing she had no choice but to keep going, Gabbie took a deep breath and approached the porch.

"Gabbie?" Mrs Carruthers squinted at her with surprise and concern. "How are you feeling?"

"I'm having another bad headache," Gabbie said. She was happy not to have to lie, for once. "I just need a couple of aspirins, and then I'll hurry back to class."

"You've had an awful lot of headaches, lately. I'm concerned about you, honey." Mrs Carruthers put down the watering can and put her hand on Gabbie's forehead. "Well, you're not running a fever."

"I'll be fine," Gabbie told her. She had an overwhelming urge to throw her arms round Mrs Carruthers and sob. To be held and comforted like a child.

Mrs Carruthers smoothed Gabbie's hair. "Still, I'm going to call over and make an appointment for you at the clinic. After what you've been through, it would put my mind at ease to know that you're not suffering – physically, at least."

Gabbie could only nod and smile weakly.

"How about four o'clock, Gabbie?"

"Fine," she murmured.

By four o'clock I'll be long gone. Where, I have no idea, but someplace where I won't hurt anyone or cause any more problems.

Gabbie suddenly felt lighter than she had in over a week. Making the decision to run away somehow made everything bearable. There was a spring in her step as she climbed the stairs to her room and she was humming to herself as she reached for her door, which was standing slightly ajar.

Cold. Unbearable cold.

Gabbie ignored it. *You, whatever you are, can't hurt me any more,* she thought as she pushed open the door. As the door swung open, she glimpsed a dark shadow above her. Then her brain exploded with pain as something heavy crashed down on her head. Gabbie fell to the floor, writhing in agony.

I'm dead, Gabbie thought. *You've killed me.*

Somewhere far away she was certain she heard a little girl's taunting laugh. Then, blessedly, she lapsed into unconsciousness.

CHAPTER ELEVEN

Neptune has slipped quietly into Gemini. You may find that you are unusually perceptive, maybe even telepathic. Sometimes that translates into poetry, or psychic ability – or madness. Hang loose. This aspect will pass. That 12th House is still quaking with unresolved unrest – dig a little deeper and you'll find the answers you're searching for.

"I'm hiding, I'm hiding. You can't find me."

"I can, too!"

"No, you can't!"

Two five-year-old girls, both in matching red dresses, chased each other round the upper floor of the big white house. Their ruffled white ankle socks and black strappy shoes matched, too. So did their raven black hair, cut chin length with a heavy fringe. The little girls were mirror images of each other.

"Genevieve is rotten," one of them cried from the top of the stairs. "She tried to hurt me. Now I'm going to make her pay for it."

Their young mother appeared at the bottom of the stairs. She was beautiful, with her long dark hair tied back in a green ribbon, her full lips outlined in red.

"Now, Gabrielle," she scolded, "it's not nice to say things like that about your sister."

"She's not Gabrielle," said the other girl, appearing next to her sister. She clutched a teddy bear in her arms. "I am."

Their mother laughed softly. "Sometimes you even fool me! Now play nicely, you two!" She disappeared, leaving the sweet scent of her perfume in the air.

Gabbie rubbed one hand over Edward the bear's head. "Genny, why do you pretend that you're me?"

Genevieve put her pudgy little hands on her hips. "So they'll think you're bad and give you away," she said matter-of-factly. "Then I'll have this house all to myself."

Gabbie slumped down against the flowered wallpaper of the upstairs hallway. She started to cry. "Genny, you are so mean."

Genevieve patted her sister on the shoulder. "Did I hurt your feelings?" Her voice sounded concerned, but her eyes were empty and cold. "I'm sorry. Would you like to go out on the balcony and play with me?"

Gabbie shook her head. "No. I don't like it there. It's too high. I'm scared."

"There's nothing to be afraid of," her sister laughed. "Hold my hand. I'll take care of you."

Gabbie stood up and smoothed her dress. She was holding tight to her stuffed bear, Edward. "Will you promise to play nicely with me?"

"Of course." Genevieve straightened the dress of her porcelain doll. "I'll even bring Emmeline and we can have a tea party."

Genevieve led Gabbie on to the balcony outside their parents' bedroom. The view seemed to go on for ever. From where they stood they could see across the lawn to the glittering bend of the Potomac river, and on into Virginia across acres of green-topped trees.

"We can see the whole wide world!" exclaimed Gabbie, flinging her arms wide with glee.

But when she turned round to look for her sister, Gabbie saw that Genevieve was closing the French windows leading back into the house.

"Don't!" she whimpered. "Genny, I want to go back in."

"Go ahead," challenged Genny. She stared at her sister with unmasked hatred. "Who's stopping you?" Suddenly she lunged at Gabbie.

Gabbie screamed. But no one heard her. She screamed again, louder. *Edward! Save me!*

Then someone was shaking her. A voice was trying to reach her. "Gabbie! Gabbie! Wake up! You're dreaming!"

Slowly Gabbie opened her eyes. Everything was white. Her head throbbed with pain.

"Thank god you're finally awake," said the voice. It belonged to Liz, who was standing next to her in the white room. "You've been sleeping for ever."

Gabbie tried to speak, but her tongue was thick and her mouth was dry. Slowly she reached up to touch her head and felt the swirl of gauze bandages.

"Where am I?" she asked very slowly, as if remembering how to speak.

"In the infirmary," whispered Liz. "I'm not going to tell the nurse you're awake – I have to talk to you first."

"Oh, Liz," Gabbie gasped. "I saw her. That little girl, in my dream!"

"What little girl?"

"The one at the funeral," Gabbie said excitedly. "And in the kitchen. I dreamed I was back at my home. Years ago. When I was a little girl."

"Shh! Calm down!" whispered Liz.

"But I'm trying to tell you about my dream!"

"Gabbie! Hush! The nurse will hear you. You won't believe this, but you were hit on the head by a breeze block. It's a wonder you're alive."

"A breeze block?" Gabbie gingerly patted the bandages on her head. "When?"

"Yesterday. You've been delirious." Liz leaned forward and tucked the sheet round Gabbie. She was wearing her riding jacket and smelled faintly of horses and fresh straw. "You can't trust your dreams."

"But tell me what happened?" Gabbie rasped.

"Yesterday afternoon when you opened the door to our room, a breeze block fell off the top and hit you on the head."

"How did it get there?" asked Gabbie. She tried to sit up but the slightest movement made her head hurt.

"Better lie still," Liz warned. "If the nurses know you're awake you'll have to start talking to people."

"But how—?"

"They think someone set a trap," Liz whispered. Her eyes were wide.

"Am I hurt – badly?" Gabbie asked. She touched her bandaged head again.

Liz hesitated. "You had concussion and some lacerations. That's why you're all bandaged. Darby found you. I guess there was blood everywhere."

"Who would do that?" Gabbie repeated. "Who would hurt me?" She grabbed Liz's hand. "Oh, Liz. I'm really scared."

Liz put her finger on her lips. Then she tiptoed to the door and peered into the hallway. When she returned, she said, "Things are worse than you think."

"How could they be any worse than this?" Gabbie reached for the glass on the bedside stand and took a sip of warm water. "Tell me. Please."

"There's talk round school that you've been making all of this up," said Liz. "Tiffany says she heard some teachers saying maybe you're schizophrenic." She looked embarrassed to be the one bringing bad news to her oldest friend.

"But what about the calls and the notes?" asked Gabbie with foggy disbelief.

Liz kept her voice calm and free of judgment. "No one ever heard the caller but you. The calls can't be verified. And they think you wrote the notes yourself."

"But it's not my handwriting," Gabbie insisted. "Surely they can see that."

Liz paused. Gabbie could tell that she was struggling.

"They think it *is* your handwriting, but written with your left hand."

"I don't believe it!" Gabbie gasped. She wanted to cry, but she knew it would hurt her head even more. "This is just insane. They can't prove that!"

"They think they have, Gabbie. Listen – maybe I should leave and let you rest. I wanted to help, but I'm just making things worse."

Gabbie clutched Liz's arm. "No! Stay, please. I have to know. You have to tell me what you know."

Liz thought for a moment and then nodded. "OK. If that's what you want."

“It’s what I want,” Gabbie whispered.

“Well,” Liz continued, “remember last year when Mr Lorton had us do those projects to free our creative spirit?”

Gabbie vaguely recalled the art teacher’s week of crazy experiments – writing to music, drawing blindfolded, drawing with one hand while writing with the other. “But what does that have to do with this?”

“Remember the exercise we did writing poems with our opposite hand?” Liz prompted. “Well, I guess Lorton kept those poems on file. The FBI compared the poems you wrote with your left hand to those notes, and—”

“They match,” Gabbie finished. Her head felt as if it was being gripped by steel bands. “Please, Liz. I swear to you, I didn’t do it. I didn’t write the notes. Why would I?”

“For attention is what they’re saying. And sympathy.”

Gabbie was astounded. “They think I’d drop a breeze block on my head for sympathy? If I wasn’t so scared, I’d have a good laugh about that.”

“The FBI man thinks one possible explanation is that you were setting a trap for someone else. That you put the breeze block there for. . . me, or Darby." Liz's voice choked. "And that you got caught in your own trap."

"No!" Gabbie shouted. "Why would I hurt you, Liz?"

"Why would you smash Colin's car window, or destroy a soccer ball in front of a bunch of little girls?" Liz frowned. "Something *has* happened to you."

Footsteps sounded outside the hospital room door. And voices. They were coming closer.

"It sounds like Albion!" Liz hissed.

"Oh, no!" said Gabbie. "What should we do?"

They both looked round frantically. "I'll get under the bed," Liz said. "You pretend to be asleep – no matter what happens. Quick!"

Gabbie pulled the sheet up higher and closed her eyes. She tried to make her breath slow and even.

The door opened and she heard the headmistress say quietly, "Here's her room." Gabbie lay still as she heard people approach her bed. "She's sleeping," Mrs Albion said. "I don't think there's any point in trying to talk to her until she's fully awake."

"I suppose you're right," said another female voice. "Though I want this wretched business concluded as soon as possible."

That voice! Aunt Louise!

"We all want this unpleasant situation to be resolved," Mrs Albion agreed. "Fairly and equitably, of course."

Gabbie heard one of them pull the white curtain round her bed. She could relax a tiny bit, now that they couldn't see her. *I just hope they don't see Liz!*

Believing Gabbie to be sound asleep, the two women began talking about her as though she wasn't there.

"It's quite amazing to discover that Gabrielle was a twin," Mrs Albion remarked.

"Yes, we lost Genevieve when she was only five."

Twin! The news hit Gabbie like a jolt of electricity. Her dream about the two matching little girls wasn't a dream after all.

"Were they identical?" asked Mrs Albion.

"As a matter of fact, they were what's known as mirror image twins. Whatever one had on the right side, the other had on the left." Aunt Louise's voice grew bitter. "They were also opposite in every way. Gabrielle was always mean-spirited – and dirty, too, making a mess wherever she went. And Genevieve, sweet Genny – she was a perfect little doll."

"How interesting," said Mrs Albion. "Gabbie's always been quite neat here at school."

"Well, obviously you've found ways to handle her here," Aunt Louise replied. "Believe me, she was a very difficult little girl, constantly fighting with her twin. My sister Susan nearly died giving birth to those girls. And from the first second they drew breath, they were rivals."

"Such a shame," murmured Mrs Albion. "I'm so surprised I never knew."

You're surprised! Gabbie wanted to shout. *What about me? I have no memory of a sister at all.*

"Susan and Nick worked very hard to keep their children out of the limelight. This was before Nick became an ambassador."

"I see."

"When Genny fell, Susan and Nick were certain Gabbie had pushed her," Aunt Louise said. "Of course, they didn't dare mention it to anyone."

Pushed her? Gabbie struggled to sit up, but Liz, hiding under the bed, reached up and slapped her arm. She forced herself to lie still on the bed.

"Bringing those suspicions out in the open would have affected Nick's career. He was a rising star in the diplomatic corps – any hint of a personal scandal would have ruined his future chances. We held a quiet funeral at home, and told the press that we wished to grieve privately."

"You truly think that a little five-year-old girl is capable of killing another child?" Mrs Albion asked. Her voice was polite but tinged with scepticism. That pleased Gabbie.

"Oh, yes! Believe me, you don't know the real Gabrielle. She's pure evil. When Gabrielle was old enough to attend White Springs, Susan and I made a pact in the family never to mention her sister or the incident again. We also agreed that we would never let that – that monster hurt Susan again."

Monster? Tears welled in the corners of Gabbie's eyes and rolled down the side of her face on to her pillow. So this was what her parents had thought of her. All those years.

Gabbie couldn't help it – a moan of absolute despair escaped her lips.

Fortunately neither woman heard. Her aunt's voice drowned her out as she exploded with rage and anguish, "And somehow that twisted creature returned and murdered her own parents! My sister!"

"You're very upset," Mrs Albion murmured, patting the sobbing woman on the back.

"Of course I'm upset," Louise cried. "All I can think of is my poor sister. And my sweet little niece lying there in that coffin. She looked like an angel, all in white, cradling her favourite doll."

Louise was crying harder now, sniffling and blowing her nose on a handkerchief. "I'm so sorry, Mrs Albion, I had no right to snap at you like that."

"I understand. Why don't we go to my office?" Mrs Albion suggested. "You can rest on the daybed for a while, and I'll get my secretary to make you some tea."

"Thank you," Louise sniffed. "You've been very kind. And I'll feel much better when that monster is locked away for ever."

"I'll instruct the nurse to alert us the moment Gabrielle is awake."

Finally, the two women left the room. Gabbie and Liz remained motionless until they heard the door click shut and the footsteps cease. Then Liz crept out from under the bed.

CHAPTER TWELVE

"Genevieve," Gabbie repeated over and over. "Genevieve."

She had left her hospital bed and was now standing in front of the mirror in the tiny bathroom, studying her reflection. Liz sat on the edge of the hospital bed, stunned by what they had learned. First, that Gabbie had a twin, and second, that the twin had died, and in the same terrible way as the Bradfords.

"Genevieve. Genevieve."

As Gabbie repeated her twin's name, a deeply buried memory began to surface in her mind. She tried to hold on to it, to bring it into focus. The images were fuzzy, like a bad photograph. She could see the balcony of her parents' house. White wicker furniture. Two little girls sitting down, a plate of cookies between them.

I have Edward with me. And Genny has Emmeline.

"Emmeline!" Gabbie said out loud, her eyes widening to become two big circles in her face.

"Gabbie." Liz looked at her friend, her eyes filled with worry and fear. "What now?"

Gabbie shuffled quickly into the room, clutching her head to try to ease the throbbing pain. "Do you remember what my aunt said about my sister?"

Just saying thc word sister still felt foreign to her.

"She said she was your mirror image. Except she was good and you were bad," Liz said, simply.

Gabbie winced at Liz's words. "Do you think that's true? You've known me since we were twelve."

Liz shook her head vehemently. "You've always been kind and considerate. OK, a little neurotic sometimes about your parents, but after what your aunt just said, I don't blame you."

Gabbie breathed a huge sigh of relief. "Now I have another question for you. This one is difficult for me to ask, but I know it's even harder for you to answer."

Liz met Gabbie's eyes with a straight,

honest clarity. "Fire away."

"Do you think I killed my parents?"

"No," Liz answered without hesitation. "For lots of reasons, but mostly because there is no way you could have driven to your parents' house and back in my car. You didn't have enough gas."

"Are you sure?"

"Absolutely. When you borrowed my car it only had an eighth of a tank of gas. You borrowed three dollars from me for shampoo. Remember?"

"Right! Because I was waiting for my weekly cash from the bursar's office."

"Yes. And when you returned the car, I remember thinking – now don't be offended – but I remember thinking at the time that just once I wished you would return my car with gas in it."

Gabbie's face flushed. "Sorry."

"It's a bad habit of yours," Liz continued. "You never, ever pay for gas. I think practically every girl at White Springs who has a car could testify to that."

"I just never thought of it," Gabbie apologized.

"Don't be embarrassed," Liz said, leaping off the bed and hugging her. "It proves that you couldn't have done it."

Gabbie smiled. "That's brilliant, Liz. But it's not enough."

"What do you mean?"

"I have to prove that I didn't kill my sister. I think they – the police, the school, my aunt – everybody thinks thc two deaths are related."

Liz put her hands on her hips. "Well, who do you think committed the murders?"

Gabbie raised her hand. "Now you're really going to think I've gone off the deep end but bear with me for a minute."

"All right."

Gabbie poured herself another glass of water and took a long swallow. "Ever since I returned to my parents home in Maryland, I've had this feeling that I'm not alone. When I was at the funeral, I thought I saw a little girl standing by the hearse. And then when we returned to Smith Hall, I was certain I saw that same little girl sitting on the chair in the kitchen."

Liz shivered. "Don't talk like that, Gabbie, you're giving me the creeps."

"Then I started receiving those notes, and

getting the phone calls, and hearing a little girl's voice taunting me. Do you remember what the notes said?"

Liz squeezed her eyes closed, trying to think. "Um, one was something like, 'It should have been you. Next time it will be.'"

Gabbie nodded. "And another said, 'You're going to pay for what you did.'"

Liz paled visibly as she grasped what Gabbie was trying to say. "You don't think. . . ?"

Gabbie nodded. "I think my dead sister somehow murdered my parents. I think – though I would never have believed it before last week – that she has come back from. . . wherever, and has been tormenting me."

"But the notes," Liz said. "The teacher said they were written in your hand."

"Yes, with my left hand. I think Genevieve has managed to get inside my head, where at times she can force me to do things – like scream at people, or write the notes, and smash Colin's window." Gabbie held out her left palm. A deep ragged cut, now scabbed over, ran down the middle, from the brick she had thrown at Colin's windshield. "Look at my left hand."

"What about it?"

"I'm right-handed. If it were me throwing that brick, I would have used my right hand. But my left is the one that got scraped."

"But how do you know your sister is left-handed?"

"Mirror image," Gabbie said. "You heard my aunt. I have a mole on my left arm. That means Genevieve's is on her right." Gabbie pulled Liz to the mirror with her. "My hair is parted on the right, so Genevieve's is parted on the left. My right foot is slightly larger than my left."

"So her left would be larger than her right."

Gabbie held up her right hand. "So if I'm right-handed—"

"Genevieve would be left-handed," Liz concluded with a nod of comprehension. "But how can you prove she's come back from the dead? I mean, you can't just call her and poof, she'll appear." Liz moved closer to Gabbie and whispered nervously, "Can you?"

"No. But there is one thing that proves that she's come back."

"What is it?"

"The doll. The one Aunt Louise was going on about. Emmeline. Remember, she said Genevieve looked like an angel all in white lying in her coffin holding her favourite doll. That doll was Emmeline."

"So what does that prove? That doll was buried with your sister."

"Exactly. And less than a week ago, I saw – and so did Agent Scharfe – that very same doll seated at the table on the balcony of my parents' house."

Liz shivered so hard this time her teeth chattered. "Oh, this really creeps me out, Gabbie. Don't talk that way."

Gabbie grabbed Liz's shoulders. "I have to say it. It's the truth." She clasped her head. "I have to get that doll. It will prove that I'm innocent."

"Do you think it's still in the house?" Liz asked.

"I don't know. But I intend to find out." Gabbie moved to the wardrobe where her school uniform from the day before had been hung. She whipped off her hospital gown and began pulling on her clothes. "Liz, I have to go back there."

"Now?"

"If I don't go now, while they all think I'm still unconscious, I'll never be allowed to leave.

You heard the way Mrs Albion and Aunt Louise were talking. They're planning to lock me up."

"But they can't do that," Liz protested. "You'd have to have a trial first. Or see a doctor, or something."

Gabbie slipped on her blazer and scoffed, "A trial. Right. They'd have everyone testify, including you, that I've been acting really weird lately. Aunt Louise would swear I murdered my sister in the exact same way that I murdered my parents. Then I would say I think the ghost of my sister did it – and that would be the end of that."

"How are you going to get there?" asked Liz. "Your head is bandaged, you're being watched every minute, you don't have a car—"

"But you do," Gabbie interrupted. "Help me, Liz. Please?"

"I don't know." Liz wrung her hands. "I don't know. How would we get out of here?"

"Through that window." Gabbie pointed to the large window across from the bed. "We're on the ground floor."

"We'll get caught," Liz protested. "Someone will see us."

"We have to try. It's my only chance. If I

don't go, they'll put me away – for ever."

Liz considered this. She looked outside the window. And then back at Gabbie. "I don't know if I believe in ghosts," she whispered. "But if they exist, I certainly don't want to see one."

"Liz, please." Gabbie knew she was begging for her life.

"Oh, geez!" Liz threw her arms in the air. "All right. Let's go. But hurry. Before I lose my nerve."

Quickly, Gabbie slipped on her shoes. She raced to the sink and splashed water on her face. As she peered at her reflection, it began to change shape. A little girl's face appeared with an ugly, twisted mouth.

"You'll never get me!" she hissed. *"Never."*

"Wanna bet?" Gabbie slammed her hand over the image in the mirror and turned away. "Come on," she told Liz. "Let's go."

Gabbie opened the window as far as she could, and detached the rusted screen. Liz crawled out, hunching down when her feet touched the pavement.

Gabbie followed. But as she ducked through the window, she felt something catch hold of her arm. *She's trying to hold me back. She knows I'm coming.*

The cold and the fear swirled inside her and black spots floated and whirled like snowflakes in front of her eyes. Gabbie moaned, feeling her will weakening. But with a mighty effort, she hissed, "No!" Her arm broke free and she jumped to the pavement beside Liz.

The two girls raced along the side of the building, heading towards the parking lot and Liz's car.

"What am I doing?" Liz muttered as she struggled to unlock her car door with trembling hands.

"Saving my life," Gabbie answered. "Saving my life."

CHAPTER THIRTEEN

It was almost dark as Gabbie and Liz sped along the highway in Liz's car. "So far so good," Gabbie said, looking out of the back window. "I don't think anyone's following us."

"Yet," Liz said flatly.

"Well, I'm sure they've discovered that I'm gone, but I doubt they'll think I'm going home."

Liz fiddled with the car radio, trying to find a soothing station. After a while she gave up. The two girls sat in silence, watching the sun fade behind them as they headed east.

"Do you remember her at all – your sister?" Liz asked after a time.

"I think I've dreamed about her, but not until today did I really remember that I had a sister." Gabbie leaned her head back against the seat. "How does someone forget another person? Especially my other half. My mirror image."

"I read somewhere that sometimes when a

person has been through a terrible experience, a trauma, their brain shuts down that part of their memory," Liz said. "It's like a survival mechanism. A way to cope with something truly terrible."

"Like the death of a twin," Gabbie murmured.

"You know what's weird?" Liz cocked her head to look at Gabbie. "That you are a Gemini, and a twin. And that, just like all of those old myths – you have all the good characteristics, and Genevieve has the dark, evil traits."

Gabbie shuddered. "I just hope I'm strong enough to deal with her. Genevieve is forceful. Extremely forceful."

"What do you mean?"

Gabbie closed her eyes and let the memories flood back. "Well, she was born first. And she didn't want me to be born. I think I remember her telling me that when she was born, she tried to push me back in."

"How could a baby do that?" Liz asked with disbelief. "Or even remember that she'd done it."

Gabbie shook her head and abruptly all of the cobwebs obscuring her memory disappeared. She remembered her past with absolute clarity. "Because Genevieve was never normal. She used to do malicious things and pretend she was me. I'd take the blame because she would threaten to break my toys and do terrible things to my pets."

"And you believed her?"

"Yes! Once when I told Mother that Genevieve was really the one who'd broken all of the good china, Genny killed my parakeet. Took a rock and smashed his head in front of me."

"Oh, my god!" Liz said. "I'm getting really scared now. I mean, this is really out of my league. Here we are, blithely going to see this supernatural demon child, without a clue as to what to do to stop her. Don't you think we should call someone to help us?"

"Who? Colin thinks I'm crazy. If we call your parents they'll tell us to go back to school. If anyone at White Springs finds out they'll send the police, who will probably lock me up in an institution."

"But – but what if she tries to hurt you?"

Gabbie frowned. "I've endured twelve years of being hated by my parents and aunt.

Memories keep rushing back all the time now, of my time with Genny – and none of them were happy. Liz, she's been hurting me my entire life."

Liz flicked on the overhead light, checking the map. "Shouldn't we be turning soon?"

"Take this exit," Gabbie said. "I think I remember that farmhouse." Liz slowed the car down and left the highway. "Now we should stay on this winding road for about five or six miles."

Through the darkness, the girls could make out the shadows of giant trees lining either side of the narrow road. The moon was almost full and although the air was damp and fresh, Liz kept the windows rolled up tight and the doors locked.

The closer they got to the house, the more tense the girls became. Liz's shoulders were hunched nearly up to her ears, and her knuckles were white from gripping the steering wheel too tightly. "Gabbie," Liz rasped. "Why do you think your sister suddenly reappeared after twelve years?"

Gabbie pursed her lips. "I think it has something to do with my parents coming back to the house. Maybe their return stirred things up."

"You think her spirit was never laid to rest?" Liz asked, as she stared unblinking at the dark stretch of road.

"I don't know." Gabbie dug in her blazer pocket for a stick of gum. She tore it in two and gave Liz half. Both girls chewed nervously. "She might have been in that house all these years, just waiting for someone to come back."

Liz put one hand to her forehead. "I can't believe we're talking seriously about ghosts and spirits."

"I know." Gabbie leaned forward and peered into the darkness. "But it is serious. Deadly serious."

"Gabbie?" Liz suddenly whispered. "You don't think – I mean, there isn't a chance that she could suddenly appear in the car, is there? Because I don't think I could handle that."

Gabbie squeezed Liz's arm. "No, she's not here. Don't worry. I always know when she's round."

"Do you think your parents knew she – her ghost – was there?"

Gabbie chewed intently on her gum. "It's

possible they got a phone call—like the ones I received. She could have pretended to be me and told them that I was coming home late that night. That would explain the three glasses of milk and the plate of my favourite cookies still on that balcony table."

"Ugh!" Liz shuddered. "But she couldn't have made herself look like you, could she?"

"I don't think she needed to. I think when they stepped out on the balcony and saw that doll, they must have had the shock of their lives. I mean, she carried that doll everywhere, and she was buried with it!"

"So... " Liz swallowed hard. "You think they were so scared that they fell off the balcony?"

"They didn't fall," Gabbie said. "The FBI agent made that very clear."

"You mean – you think your sister pushed both of them?"

Just as Gabbie was about to respond, thcy heard a siren and saw a flash of blue and red lights behind them.

"It's the police," Liz cried.

Gabbie nearly hit her head on the ceiling trying to turn round and peer over the headrest on her seat. "Oh, no!"

"What should I do?" Liz cried.

"Pull over. We don't have a choice." Gabbie's heart was pounding.

Liz slowed the car and pulled over to the side of the road. After a minute, a uniformed officer approached the car. Liz rolled down the window with her left hand while Gabbie held tightly to her right.

The officer shone a flashlight into their car. "Evening, ladies," he said.

"Good evening, sir," Liz responded, using her best White Springs manners.

"May I see your licence and registration, please?"

Liz dug in her bag, while Gabbie stared straight ahead. By now, Agent Scharfe and the staff at White Springs would have probably alerted the police of her disappearance. This officer probably had been given a description of Liz's car and recognized it. *It's all over now.*

The officer looked at Liz's licence, and then at her.

"This vehicle is registered to a Mr and Mrs Dennis Sutton of Philadelphia, Pennsylvania. Those your folks?"

"Yes, sir," Liz answered.

"You girls are a long way from home."

"Well, sir, we go to school at White Springs Academy," Liz said, looking furtively at Gabbie. "And I'm giving my roommate here a ride home to see her – her sister. You see, she's injured her head and she's going home to rest."

The officer looked at Gabbie, and for the first time she remembered that her head was bandaged.

"Looks like you've been in the wars," he said, wincing in sympathy.

"Actually, I fell off of a horse at school." Gabbie raised one hand to pat the bandage. "It's not as bad as it looks."

The officer continued to stare at the girls. Finally, he handed Liz's licence and registration back to her. "The reason I stopped you, Miss Sutton, is—"

He stepped back for a second, scratching his head, then continued talking with a totally befuddled look on his face. "I could have sworn your left rear tail light was out, but it seems just fine now." He frowned at the light. "That's odd."

Gabbie and Liz slowly turned to look at each other and gasped, "Genevieve."

"She's trying to keep us from getting there," Gabbie whispered. "Well, it won't work."

"There might be a short in that light, Miss Sutton," the policeman said, flipping the cover on his pad closed. "I'd have it looked at, just in case."

"Thank you, officer," Liz said, forcing a smile. "I will."

The officer smiled for the first time. "Drive safely, you two. And stay off horses." He walked away, the gravel crunching under his boots.

Liz and Gabbie sat in silence until the officer had driven off. Then Liz said, shakily, "Are you sure you don't want to turn back? It's not too late."

Gabbie shook her head firmly. "We've come this far. We can't turn back." Gabbie pointed in the distance. "I'm sure the house is just up the road."

"I don't know if I can go through with this, Gabbie," Liz said, pulling her car back on the road. "I don't think I have enough courage."

"Oh, Liz, you have guts enough for both of us," Gabbie replied. Then she spotted a small sign on a mailbox that read BRADFORD.

"There!" she cried. "Take your next left. That's the driveway."

Liz turned the car on to the long driveway leading up to the darkened house. The outline of the mansion loomed starkly against the moonlit sky. "I don't like this," she chanted over and over. "I really don't like this."

Just as Liz braked the car to a stop in front of the broad porch, Gabbie was hit by a shock so forceful that it threw her back against the car seat.

Liz gripped Gabbie's arm. "What's the matter?"

"She's here," Gabbie whispered. "I can feel her."

CHAPTER FOURTEEN

"Do you want to stay in the car?" Gabbie asked Liz.

"No way!" said Liz. "I'm too scared to stay out here by myself. I'll take my chances inside with you."

The two girls stared up at the house. "I guess we'd better go, then," Gabbie said. Her mouth was so dry, she could barely swallow. She reached for her bear that rested on the seat beside her.

"You're not going to take that bear?" Liz asked. "He'll only get in the way."

"Edward has been with me since the beginning," Gabbie replied, opening her car door. "If this is the end, I want him with me."

"God, Gabbie," Liz hissed, sliding out Gabbie's side of the car. She was too afraid to get out on her side. "Don't even think that."

The girls linked arms and approached the

house. As they walked, Gabbie instinctively looked up to the balcony outside her parents' bedroom. The police tape was gone, and she could just see the outlines of the wicker table and chairs.

"Do you have keys?" Liz whispered as they reached the front door.

"No," Gabbie replied. "But I have a funny feeling I won't need a key." She turned the door knob, and the door swung open easily.

They stepped cautiously inside. Gabbie found the light switch and instantly the dark rooms were flooded with light. Things looked pretty much as they had the day of the funeral.

"That's better," Liz gasped, relieved to be in the light. "Do you mind if we just check to see if the phone works? It would make me feel a lot better to know we can call out if we need to."

They tiptoed into the study off of the living room. Gabbie turned on more lights, then picked up the receiver of the black telephone on the desk. "It works!" she cried.

"That's a relief," Liz whispered. "So – now what?"

"I have to go upstairs and get that doll," Gabbie replied. "If you want, you could wait down here by the phone."

"Not on your life!" Liz tightened her grip on Gabbie's arm. "I'm coming with you."

The girls approached the stairs but at the first step, Liz dug her nails into Gabbie's arm. "Can you hear that?"

Gabbie stopped mid-step and listened. "Yes!"

A little girl's voice echoed through the empty house. "I'm hiding, I'm hiding, and you can't find me!"

"It's her!" Gabbie said. "Genevieve."

"Uh-oh." Liz's legs buckled at the knees and Gabbie had to hold up her friend. "I think I'm going to faint."

"Liz, don't!" Gabbie pinched her friend hard. "Fainting won't help anything."

As abruptly as the chanting started, it stopped.

"Has she gone?" Liz moaned.

Gabbie shook her head. "I know you're up there, Genevieve," she called. "And I'm coming to get you."

"No! Wait," Liz pleaded. "I've changed my mind. Let's go home, Gabbie. Please, please let's go."

Gabbie was determined to go through with it. "There's no turning back, Liz. Not now."

Liz buried her face in Gabbie's shoulder, getting her body as close as possible. The two of them climbed the stairs. With each step the thudding of Gabbie's heart got louder and louder. By the time she reached the landing it was like thunder rumbling in her ears.

"Genevieve, make-believe," Gabbie chanted. "You've got boogers on your sleeve."

"Do not!"

A little dark-haired girl in a white dress appeared in the shadows.

"There she is," Gabbie whispered to Liz.

Liz raised her head as the little girl stepped into the light of the stairs. Suddenly the air rang with screaming. Bloodcurdling, ear-splitting screams that rattled the brass light fixture hanging above the stairs. The voices belonged to Gabbie and Liz, who stared in horrified shock at the little girl in the rotting white dress. Bits of decayed flesh hung off her bones. She turned her head and the worms, wriggling in and out of her eye sockets, slipped on to the rug at the two girls' feet.

Liz, still screaming, the tendons of her neck

looking ready to burst, fell backwards. She tumbled over and over and over until she landed at the bottom of the stairs with a loud thump.

"Liz!" Gabbie cried, not daring to take her eyes off the ghoulish figure in front of her. "Are you all right?"

She was answered by a low moan.

"Run, Liz!" Gabbie shrieked. "Get to the phone. Get help!"

The rotting corpse's mouth opened, releasing a foul stench as it hissed, "That should have been you!"

Gabbie covered her mouth and nose, trying hard not to vomit. This must have been what her parents had seen that night on the balcony. She gripped the stair rail, trying to remember her purpose – to get that doll.

Genevieve's ghostly image wavered and then disappeared. Gabbie heard a thud from somewhere near her parents' room. She knew she had to follow.

"Get out of this house, Liz," Gabbie rasped over her shoulder. "Crawl if you have to. Just get out. Now!"

Still clutching Edward, Gabbie willed herself to follow her sister. She went into her parents' bedroom. The French windows were standing open, the lace curtains fluttering gently in the breeze. Outside, set up for a perfect tea party, was the little wicker table and chairs. Seated at the table was the doll, her porcelain face still perfect, unchanged.

"Emmeline," Gabbie whispered.

Suddenly Genevieve appeared in the door, looking very much the perfect girl from Gabbie's memory. "Don't you dare touch Emmy. She's mine."

Gabbie realized with a shock that her sister was still a child. A very clever little girl of five.

"I don't want your doll," Gabbie said. "I have Edward the bear. He's much nicer than a rotting old doll."

"Is not!" Genevieve's nostrils flared. "Your bear is stupid. Look at him, he doesn't even have an arm. Emmeline is much nicer than Edward ever was."

Gabbie took a chance and turned her back on her sister. "How would I know that if you won't let me touch her?"

Genevieve hesitated. "Well. . . maybe just one little touch. Just so you can see how truly wonderful she is." She grinned. "Mommy bought her specially for me. You didn't deserve a doll so you got a lumpy old bear."

Gabbie turned back, trying to not let her eagerness show. She moved ever so casually towards the table. "I don't know if I want to touch that doll," she said, rocking Edward in her arms.

"Oh, go ahead." Genevieve followed her to the little wicker table. The closer Gabbie got to Emmeline, the more she realized that the doll had really been rotting underground for twelve years. The little doll's white dress was completely stained with mildew, and the pretty lace collar almost completely eaten away.

Gabbie took a deep breath. *It's now or never.*

She lunged for the doll as headlights flashed across the upstairs balcony. *What?* Gabbie, clutching Edward and Emmeline to her chest, spun to see who could possibly be coming down the drive.

"Big mistake!" Genevieve shrieked.

Suddenly Gabbie felt herself being propelled by a fierce force towards the balcony railing. She burst through in a shower of splintering wood. Gabbie desperately grasped at the metal girder attaching the balcony to the side of the house. As she dangled helplessly from the broken rail, the final pieces of her memory came back to her.

The two little girls were back at the tea party. Suddenly, Genevieve shut the French windows.

"Let me out," Gabbie pleaded. "I'm scared."

"Nobody's stopping you," Genny taunted.

As Gabbie moved to leave, Genny swung the door open, smashing Gabbie against the railing. Genny took the door and slammed it into Gabbie again and again.

"Stop!" Gabbie tried to cry. But the wind had been knocked out of her. "Please."

Genny slammed the door until the railing finally gave way, and Gabbie tumbled backwards. Still clutching Edward, Gabbie reached out for her sister, whose head was thrown back in hysterical laughter.

Edward's head caught between the rails, stopping Gabbie with a bone-jarring jolt. Gabbie dangled above the path, too terrified to even breathe.

Suddenly Genevieve's face appeared over the railing. "I thought I'd got rid of you," she hissed between clenched teeth. "It's that bear!"

Gabbie watched helplessly as her sister

straddled the rail and struggled to pry the bear loose. She pounded on Gabbie's knuckles, screaming, "Let go!"

But Gabbie would not let go. And Edward did not come loose.

Mustering all her strength, Genny grabbed the bear's arm and wrenched it out of its socket with such force that she fell backwards off the railing.

The last thing Gabbie remembered of her sister was her look of stunned surprise as she slipped out of sight and plummeted to the concrete path below.

In the distance, Gabbie vaguely heard car doors slam and footsteps scramble across the gravel driveway. The memory from the past cleared and she struggled to maintain her precarious grip. Horrified voices shouted up at her, "Hang on! Don't let go!"

Once again, Gabbie's sister hovered above her. "Too late," Genevieve hissed, her fetid breath fouling the air. "They're too late."

Genevieve picked up one of the wicker chairs and held it menacingly above her head.

"What about Emmeline!" Gabbie cried out. "You don't want to hurt Emmy!"

While Edward the bear had fallen into the darkness, Genevieve's doll was caught between Gabbie and the railing. "If I go," Gabbie whispered, "Emmeline goes. I'd hate to see her head shatter into a million pieces."

Genevieve lowered the chair. "Give me my doll," she said, reaching one ghostly hand to Gabbie."

"Here she is. Here's your doll." With all her remaining strength, Gabbie tightened her grip on the railing. And with the other hand, she hurled the doll into the darkness. "Go and get her!"

The ghost shrieked and lunged for Emmeline. Gabbie heard the doll's head shatter as it hit the path. It was followed by a piercing scream – and then silence.

Gabbie watched numbly as her fingers lost their strength. "And now I'm going to die. First Genny, and then—"

Suddenly strong hands grabbed her wrists. Her body was pulled up over the railing on to the balcony. Voices babbled incoherently round her. Her head pulsed beneath the bandages.

I'm still alive, Gabbie thought in amazement. Then she collapsed in a dead faint.

CHAPTER FIFTEEN

Gabbie closed the small brown overnight case with a final click. She had finished packing. Allowed to take anything from her parents' home, Gabbie had chosen one photo from her father's study. She had her clothes, that picture and Edward, her beloved bear.

A knock on the study door startled Gabbie. She still jumped at every sound. "Come in," she called.

Agent Scharfe opened the door. "Are you ready to go?" he asked.

"I think so," she said. "There's not a lot I want to take with me."

"I don't blame you." He gestured over his shoulder to the living room. "The carpenters are here, at your request, to board up the house."

"Good," Gabbie said firmly. "The sooner this place is closed up, the better."

"Look." Agent Scharfe gestured to the the window, overlooking the backyard and the

Potomac. "The sun's coming out."

Gabbie moved to the window. It was true. The sky was a hazy, spring blue. "That's a relief. It's been raining non-stop since the day my parents died."

Agent Scharfe stepped into the study, pulling the door closed behind him. "Look," he murmured, confidentially, "I still don't know what it was I saw last night, but I just want you to know it was enough to convince me that you didn't kill your parents."

"But you weren't the only one who saw Genevieve," Gabbie reminded him. "Liz and Aunt Louise saw her, too."

"Yes, well, your aunt is still under sedation," the agent said. "But she, also, is convinced of your innocence." Agent Scharfe scratched his head. "It was seeing that doll that did it. The shock sent her right off the deep end."

Gabbie pursed her lips. "We have a lot to talk about, my aunt and I. Some day."

"I gather she's been pretty hard on you."

"Yes," said Gabbie, looking evenly at the agent. "All of you have. You, my aunt, the headmistress. The only person who believed me was Liz."

"Oh, speaking of Liz," Agent Scharfe said, "she left you a message." He reached into his pocket and pulled out several slips of paper. "Let's see. There's one from Mrs Albion. One from your roommate Darby. Two from Mr and Mrs Sutton. And one from Colin."

"Colin! He called me?"

Agent Scharfe nodded. "He wondered what you were doing Saturday night."

Gabbie smiled. Maybe the sun really was coming out after all.

The FBI agent continued to dig in his pockets. "Shoot, I thought her message was round here someplace. Anyway, Liz said – " He rolled up his eyes, trying to remember the exact wording. "Her ankle's fine, just a simple fracture. And her ribs weren't broken, only bruised. However, her hair has turned completely white from fright."

Gabbie threw back her head and laughed. "That's my Liz, cracking jokes all the way to the hospital."

"Yes." Agent Scharfe nodded. "She is really something!"

"So will you continue to work on the case?" Gabbie asked, picking up her suitcase and moving to the door.

"Not me," he said, shoving his hands in his pockets. "I'm closing the book on this one. We may never know who killed your parents. . . "

I know who did it. We all know. Only you can't write "ghost" on an FBI report.

"But you can rest assured that you've been cleared."

"Thanks," Gabbie said. "I'm anxious to return to White Springs, and a normal life."

The two of them left the study and walked towards the living room. "So can I ask you a question?" Gabbie said to the agent. "How did you know to come here last night?"

"Well. . . " He scratched his head again. "I was visiting a friend at the local police station, when a call came over the wire. The policeman reported stopping two girls in a white sedan on a back road in Maryland."

"And you knew it was us from that description?"

"He added that one had a bandaged head, the other was wearing riding gear, and there was a beat-up teddy bear sitting between them." He grinned at her. "It was the bear that gave you away."

"The bear!" Gabbie shook her head in

amazement. "That's twice that little stuffed animal has saved my life. Once, when my sister was alive, and then again last night."

Agent Scharfe leaned towards Gabbie. "I never believed in ghosts – before."

"Me neither."

"Is she—?" He glanced nervously over his shoulder at the staircase. "Do you think she's still here?"

Gabbie listened for a minute to the sounds in the old house. She took a mental inventory of her own body. *No feeling of coldness. No headache – even under these bandages. No sense of something wrong.*

"No," Gabbie said. "I don't think so. I can't feel her any more."

The agent definitely looked relieved.

Footsteps crunched on the gravel driveway outside and Gabbie hurried to look out of the picture window. "Look, it's Liz and her parents. And they're on time!"

"Are they taking you back to school?"

"First they're taking me home to Pennsylvania for a long weekend."

"You look like you could use a rest," the agent said.

Gabbie smiled. "I'm going to sleep for a week."

After Gabbie exchanged hugs with Liz and her parents, and said goodbye to Agent Scharfe, she turned and looked back at the house for one final farewell.

Goodbye, Mom and Dad. Goodbye, Genevieve. And goodbye, unhappiness.

Gabbie settled into the back seat of the Suttons'car next to Liz. The girls squeezed hands, but they didn't talk.

There will be plenty of time for talk, later. Right now I'm going to lean back, close my eyes, and enjoy the feeling of being safe and sound with people who love me.

The car pulled away. As the workers began boarding up the Bradford house, a tiny figure dressed in white stood at the topmost window, rocking something in her arms.

*ARIES*TAURUS*GEMINI*CANCER*LEO*VIRGO*LIBRA*
*SCORPIO*SAGITTARIUS*CAPRICORN*AQUARIUS*PISCES*

Twelve signs of the Zodiac. Twelve novels, each one embracing the characteristics of a zodiac sign. Pushed to the extreme, these characteristics lead down twisting paths into tales of mystery, horror, romance and fantasy.

Whatever your sun sign, you will want to read Zodiac, the series written in the stars.

ARIES	SECRET IDENTITY
TAURUS	BLACK OUT
GEMINI	MIRROR IMAGE
CANCER	DARK SHADOWS
LEO	STAGE FRIGHT
VIRGO	DESPERATELY YOURS
LIBRA	FROZEN IN TIME
SCORPIO	DEATH GRIP
SAGITTARIUS	STRANGE DESTINY
CAPRICORN	DON'T LOOK BACK
AQUARIUS	SECOND SIGHT
PISCES	SIXTH SENSE

SERIES CREATED BY JAHNNA N. MALCOLM

VIRGO:
PERFECTIONIST, ORDERLY
DESPERATELY YOURS

Virginia is always in control, so when disturbing letters arrive at her school newspaper office from someone signed Desperate, it is Virginia who deals with them. But when a friend dies, a photograph is maliciously destroyed and the letters from Desperate become more threatening... Virginia's orderly world is tested to the limit.

LIBRA:
FAIR-MINDED, ROMANTIC
FROZEN IN TIME

Lily lives for her painting. With her boyfriend, she creates a mural that grows ever more beautiful as her own life becomes harsher. Then her boyfriend is killed by a gang. Has Lily lost him forever? If only she could be with him still in the beautiful world of the painting...

AQUARIUS:
INDEPENDENT, INNOVATIVE
SECOND SIGHT

Amber has always been different. She discovers that she has special powers that frighten her. Her dreams about other people come true - with dramatic results. Can she really control other people's lives? Can she control her own? When disaster strikes at a rodeo, Amber's powers are put to the test.

ARIES:
FIERY, DETERMINED
SECRET IDENTITY

Alex is a great musician. She's also a girl. Frustrated at not being taken seriously, Alex disguises herself as a boy, and it works - too well. Her band is a hit but if it becomes even more successful, will she be stuck as a boy forever?